"'SCUSE ME, MISS, BUT HOW MUCH?"

Hidden from view, Ki stood in a darkened doorway, his muscles tensed and ready to pounce. His ears straining to hear what was said, he held his breath and waited.

The man dug deep into his overcoat pocket. A gloved hand produced two shiny coins. "Here. Now we go?"

Jessie tossed the coins casually into her handbag, her senses taut. This could be the one. In silence the two headed for her rooms. While they walked, Jessie's mind raced as she tried to sense if this were the slasher.

Once inside, Jessie made a big thing of locking the front door behind her. She knew Ki had slipped in by the back door and would be waiting in the kitchen. She took off her cape and bonnet and eyed the customer provocatively. He averted his eyes and removed his gloves, keeping his hat, coat, and muffler on. He stuffed the gloves into his overcoat pockets and placed his portmanteau on the bed.

As he clicked the suitcase locks open, Ki prepared to spring forward. This would be it—the man was going for his scalpel. He flung back the suitcase lid and reached under the clothing. Ki sucked in a deep breath and jumped. . . .

WESLEY ELLIS

LONE STAR

AND THE RIPPER

JOVE BOOKS, NEW YORK

LONE STAR AND THE RIPPER

A Jove Book/published by arrangement with
the author

PRINTING HISTORY
Jove edition/May 1990

ISBN: 0-515-10309-8

Jove Books are published by The Berkley Publishing Group,
200 Madison Avenue, New York, New York 10016.
The name ''JOVE'' and the ''J'' logo are trademarks belonging
to Jove Publications, Inc.

PRINTED IN THE UNITED STATES OF AMERICA

10   9   8   7   6   5   4   3   2   1

Chapter 1

Daisy Dudler's feet hurt. She stood on one foot and then the other, wriggling her toes, trying to make the pain go away. Drawing her shawl tightly around bare shoulders, she sighed and saw her breath in the night air. She shivered and glanced down the street, hoping to see someone who would join her in a little body heat for a price. A carriage went by, both horse's and driver's breath visible against the yellow streetlamps.

It was much too cold to be out, she thought, trying to convince herself that the cash in her handbag was enough for one night. Hadn't she just enjoyed a long and lusty evening with her regular Wednesday-night gentleman? Did she really need to roam the streets of St. Louis in search of one last customer?

No! she decided, almost aloud. She turned on her heel to go home and bumped into someone close at hand.

"Oh, 'scuse me!" she said, looking up into a shadowy face backlit by gaslight. "I didn't hear you comin'."

"Too cold to be out at this hour," came a husky voice in a cloud of frigid air. "May I escort you home, my little one?"

She looked down and said coyly, "Fer a price . . ." She watched as a gloved hand dug into a trouser pocket and reemerged. She held out her hand as three coins clinked into her palm.

"Enough?"

"Yes, sir!"

Daisy dropped the money into her handbag, took the proffered arm with a "Don't mind if I do," and led her customer to her apartment, keeping her shiny red lips closed tightly as she smiled. No sense scaring him off with her discolored teeth, she thought. She batted her mascaraed lashes, fluffed her massive red curls, and giggled.

In her most ladylike fashion, she dug into her purse, withdrew the latchkey to the front door, and handed it to her escort. From the expensive clothing and fancy black leather satchel, she was sure this would be a high-paying gentleman. Her imagination went wild, hoping he might be as generous as her dear Wednesday-night gentleman. This one had already given her three times as much as most, but she hoped there might be a tip afterward, like with Louie. But two wealthy regulars on one night would be too much to wish for.

Daisy giggled again in anticipation as her escort turned the latchkey and opened the door. She rushed by to turn up the gaslight.

"Not too bright," her customer whispered, turning back to shut and lock the door.

"That's all right with me, sweetcakes. The softer the lights, the harder the . . ." She licked her lips and looked enticingly over her shoulder as she dropped her shawl and unlaced her bodice. Pointing to a porcelain basin and pitcher on a stand next to her embroidered dressing screen, she said, "You can wash yourself over there."

She stepped out of her petticoats, sat on the edge of the bed, and undid her shoes, wriggling her thankful toes as she released them. Lying on her back, she pointed a shapely leg toward the ceiling. She knew her long legs were her most attractive feature—much longer than they should be for one as short as she was—and she always made the most

2

of them. She slowly rolled down first one stocking and then the other, flexing her toes invitingly, just in case she had an audience.

As she suspected, she was being watched. She giggled again and smiled, her brown eyes twinkling as she studied what she could see of the face that seemed to leer at her. Of course, it was hard to tell, with that hat pulled down, its wide brim casting a dark shadow. She was tired of men who wanted to keep their hats on while doing it. Daisy drew the line at shoes and hats.

This one seemed to hesitate. Most of her clients couldn't wait to get out of their clothes; some even ripped them off, others unbuttoned themselves slowly, savoring the moment. He must be new at this, she thought, seeing fingers fumble. She was pleased—there was nothing she loved more than a first-timer. How delicious he would be, almost enjoyable. Her juices flowed unexpectedly as she waited for her inexperienced customer to disrobe.

Daisy watched in wonder at the apparent embarrassment; her customer had slipped behind the dressing screen. None of her customers had ever undressed behind the screen before, but there was always a first time for everything. *How sweet!* she thought.

Daisy spread her waist-length red hair out onto the pillow and posed, rust-colored curls framing her pale flesh. She knew this always added to her customers' pleasure, and added to her price. Her full breasts peeked out from her sheer negligee, and she pointed her leg ceilingward again and massaged her firm thigh with a sensual sigh.

Her young customer was almost undressed, each garment folded neatly and placed over the chair next to the screen.

"Take your time, sweetcakes," she purred reassuringly. "Your little Daisy kin hardly wait, but we got all night." She ground her behind into the mattress and massaged her other thigh.

3

A tentative hand reached out from behind the screen and grabbed the satchel. Daisy blinked. What was in that leather bag—some sort of sexual toy? She hoped he wasn't depraved or perverted. She didn't mind unusual sex, not unless it became painful. But how strange could this young man be? She waited, squirming her hips as she stared at the screen.

The satchel clicked open. She waited. What did he have in store for her?

"Come here, Daisy."

"Take your hat off first," she said sweetly. "It'll only get in the way."

Daisy slipped off the bed and stopped at the edge of the screen, pulling open her negligee, baring her pert breasts.

"Beautiful. Now turn around."

He's either being romantic or he's going to be perverted, she thought as she faced the bed and dropped the negligee to the floor. She envisioned his nude physique as she sensed body heat of naked flesh approach. As her last customer of the evening pulled her long tresses aside, Daisy shuddered. Her one weakness was kisses on the shoulder and neck, and she drew in a deep breath in anticipation.

Just then, she remembered her bureau mirror. Glancing at it, she could see her own shapely nude figure clearly. Her eyes were drawn to the fullness of her breasts. A tinge of pride flashed through her as her eyes focused on something else in the reflection. Something bright, shiny—sharp!

She tried to turn, to struggle, but a determined arm encircled her, pinning her arms to her sides. Unable to tear her eyes from the scene being played out in the mirror, she saw something she had not expected—would never have imagined in her wildest nightmares. An insane realization of her situation surged through her as she took in as much of her assailant as she could see.

In horror Daisy Dudler watched in the mirror as her young

4

customer's hand ran something sharp across her throat. There was almost no pain, but her mouth opened in an aborted scream just as everything dimmed. The last thing she saw was the glint of a blade. She didn't see the sudden gush of blood spurt from her neck, spraying the room a vivid scarlet.

The room was silent. There had been no scream, no noise—no problem. That was good. There would be no alarm raised. The murderer's heart thumped brutally as Daisy's body slumped to the floor in a widening pool of blood. Her red hair paled by comparison to the darkened fluids.

The murderer laid Daisy's body flat on its back and knelt. Expert fingers clasped the shiny scalpel and made a bold incision from breastbone to pubic area. Sure hands scooped Daisy's intestines out and placed them on her shoulder, covering her left breast. Swiftly the scalpel sliced again and again, as Daisy's uterus and ovaries were neatly removed one by one and placed off to the side.

"There! That's that!" the killer said with pride. The excised organs were arranged and rearranged precisely. "That's better." A grin of satisfaction spread across pale lips and a low chuckle died slowly.

Taking care not to step in the blood, bare feet headed to the washbasin. Deft fingers bathed off blood, cleansed the scalpel, and replaced it in its indented place in the satchel. There was no hurry, but it would never do to become overly confident. Logic argued that at any moment, someone could come barging in. But it was far into the night and the world was asleep.

I'd better not forget anything! The thought was superfluous as clothes were quickly fastened and shoes and hat replaced. A thorough look about the room added assurance. Everything was as it should be. There was no reason to stay longer, although the great pleasure of a job well done swelled the soul, and the temptation to linger and gloat was all-consuming.

The murderer looked down smugly at the sprawled carcass, examined every detail of the brilliant surgery, and chuckled again. There would be no mistaking that handiwork. The authorities would have to take notice.

Unlocking the door, the killer peered out. No one was about. The hallway was empty in both directions and snoring rattled through the thin walls. It was so easy to slip out, lock the door, push the latchkey back under the locked door, and walk off into the night unnoticed. So easy. The backdoor to the apartment house stood unlocked, and the alley behind led directly to the next street over.

Easier than I thought it'd be! A low laugh bordering on hysteria bounced off doors and walls down the alleyway as the shadow of the murderer drifted off into the night.

Chapter 2

Hiram Carstairs gulped and tried to control his revulsion. The stench was intense, but he had smelled death and rotting flesh before. A handkerchief over the face usually took care of the smell until he could get out into the fresh air. The profuse bleeding and resultant splatters were nothing new; he had seen men shot in the throat gush rivers before dying.

But never in his twenty-seven years in police work had he seen a more gruesome murder. Someone had slit the young redhead's throat from ear to ear and then given her what appeared to be a hysterectomy. This was no crime of passion, no heat-of-the-moment violence. This was cold-blooded, calculated, crazy.

Christ! What a way to end the week! he thought. He had hoped to spend the weekend bathing and clipping his hounds—but this case was more than Detective Captain Bernard could handle alone. Chief Carstairs wanted to oversee it himself, but there went the weekend. When the call came in that a whore had been mutilated, his first instinct had been to hand it over to Curt and leave it at that. But when the patrolman mentioned innards spread out neatly, he'd reconsidered. Anyway, Curt was up to his ears in that smash-and-grab murder downtown.

"Chief, I think I found something," a half-shaven policeman said, pointing out into the hallway. He cocked his head toward the door. "Out in the hall. One of the neighbors saw the victim come home late Wednesday night."

Chief Carstairs turned quickly and headed for the door. Any excuse to leave the room for a moment. Faced with a crowd of curious bystanders, he called, "Well, Hobbs, who? Where? Which one? Come on. I don't have all day!"

The scruffy police sergeant scurried out into the packed walkway and shoved several people aside. One white-haired old woman with a long purple sash tied in her curls and a red satin robe barely covering her sagging body stared at the police chief expectantly as the others backed off.

"Here, chief. This here is Mrs. Doo—" He glanced at the woman and waited.

Fake eyelashes batting, the aging woman interrupted. "Agnes Doolittle, sir. And I seen the whole thing, I did. You may remember me from the old days at the Variety. Flannery and Doolittle, song and dance?" She did a little jig, her wilted bosoms flapping.

Chief Carstairs looked at her vacantly. "Yeah, fine. And what did you see—when was it, Wednesday night?"

Undaunted, Agnes persisted. "Harry and I toured all the East Coast, from New York to Chicago. We was—"

"Miss Doolittle, please. I got a murder here to take care of. We can reminisce another time. But for now, let's just stick to what you saw Wednesday night, if you don't mind."

She looked from Chief Carstairs to Sergeant Hobbs and back, adjusted her robe, and said, "Well, about two in the morning Wednesday night—which'd be Thursday morning, o' course—I heard Daisy coming home with someone."

Chief Carstairs asked, "Are you sure it wasn't Tuesday or Thursday? What makes you so sure it was Wednesday?"

"If you'd let me finish, I'll be tellin' you!" she shot back. She squinted and continued, "I remember thinking to myself that it was kinda strange, her coming in so late

8

after having just finished with her Wednesday gentleman. Much after two-thirty, it was, and she usually just goes out for a stroll and comes home alone. But when I heard two people tippy-toeing in, I figured she musta got lucky.'' She shook her head and looked around to make sure her audience had grasped her story. ''She got real lucky, didn't she?''

''Go on, Miss Doolittle. How did you know it was two-thirty?'' the police chief asked to get her back on track.

She smiled, and so did half the people in the hallway. ''Why, sir, I know what time each of my girls comes in. Hell, they're all so dear to my heart, I jest can't get to sleep till I know they're all safe.'' She glanced from face to face, as all the young women in the hall nodded.

''Yes, I understand,'' Chief Carstairs said.

''And, o' course, I jest wanted to see how much Daisy was gonna get from her last customer for the night, so I popped open my door jest a crack. Figured I'd size 'im up b'fore I dozed off.'' She smiled self-righteously, showing a picket-fence grin. ''He wasn't all that big—bigger'n Daisy, o' course, but half the world's bigger than poor little Daisy, rest 'er soul. Sort of average, I'd guess.'' She stared off, as if trying to remember. ''I was certain she'd struck it rich, cuz I could see he was dressed like a real gent.''

The old woman's raspy cackle caromed down the corridor, and she came close to losing control. Chief Carstairs realized the irony of her words just as she had. The old woman hacked deeply, snorted, bringing up phlegm and spitting it off to the side.

''A gent! What gent would do that! God only knows! How could anyone—''

''Thank you, Miss Doolittle,'' Chief Carstairs jumped in. ''But if this all happened Wednesday, and you watch over 'your girls' so closely, why didn't you find Daisy's body before this? You must have noticed she was missing.''

9

"Hell, no!" Indignance blazed from her watery eyes. "With a fancy gent like that, when she didn't answer the door the next morning, I jest figured she musta gone off with him." She daubed at her eyes with a brown-stained hankie, then brought it to her nose and honked loudly. "I knew she'd be back for the weekend crowd, and if not, then definitely in time for her Wednesday-night gentleman."

The young women clustered around all nodded.

"But when I smelled that awful stink coming from her room, I knew something was wrong. The door was locked, so I called the copper."

"Yes," Chief Carstairs said, glancing at Sergeant Hobbs, "the door was locked, wasn't it?"

The police sergeant nodded.

Turning back to the old woman, Chief Carstairs asked, "Is there anything else you can remember that might help us? How old was the man you saw with Daisy? Did you recognize him? Can you describe him in more detail?"

"He weren't nobody I ever saw b'fore. He was youngish, thin, wiry. Hard to tell if I knew him, what with his hat pulled way down and his collar up." She thought for a moment, her watery gray eyes fading. Then she brightened. "Oh, yes. I nearly forgot something. He was a doctor—I remember thinking to myself that maybe Daisy was gonna top the evening off right with another rich one."

"A doctor? How did you know he was a doctor if you didn't recognize him?" Chief Carstairs asked.

"He was carrying one of them black leather bags that doctors carry, o' course." She beamed, waiting for praise.

"Thank you," Chief Carstairs said abruptly as he wheeled and lumbered back into the murder victim's room, leaving Agnes Doolittle gaping. He stood looking down at the blood-spattered body, then turned to Sergeant Hobbs. "Get this cleaned up and meet me back at the station." He shoved his way out the door and down the hall.

In the carriage on his way back to police headquarters, Chief Carstairs thought matters over carefully and decided to hand the case back to Captain Bernard. Someone had overreacted. Nothing ominous here—probably just an overzealous customer. It may have appeared a little bizarre, but it was nothing earth-shattering, nothing Curt and his boys couldn't handle. The hounds needed care and clipping, and Curt was perfectly capable of dealing with both the jewelry store and the whore.

Pearl Greenwood splashed herself with water and toilet water, cleaning up after her last customer. She gazed dreamily at the gold coin on her dresser, her thoughts racing ahead to the potentials this new steady customer might bring. The possibilities were endless.

Her naked reflection in the full-length mirror caught her eye, and she grinned openly at her flawless body and sculptured features. Her preacher father had tried to drum into her head that "pride goeth before a fall," but she whisked the thought aside as she admired herself. Playfully, she brought the long blond tresses forward over her shoulders, hiding her large breasts. Her father had filled her with tales of fallen women, and her favorite was Lady Godiva, who showed off her naked body to an entire town, with only her flowing golden hair to cover her. As Pearl stood at the mirror, she pretended to be that gorgeous woman riding through town in her altogether.

Pearl jumped at the unexpected knock at the door, and she instinctively reached for her robe. For a fraction of a second she felt as if her father were about to rebuke her—but Father was dead, and she reckoned she had done nothing wrong.

"Who's there?" she called out as she went to the door.

Another knock was her only answer.

"Is that you, sweetie?" she asked sensuously. "Did you forget something?"

Yet another rap on the door.

Pearl flung open the door to see a stranger, hat pulled down, collar up, and hand extended with three bright coins sitting on a suede-gloved palm. She barely took her eyes off the coins as she cooed, "For me?" and ushered in her new customer.

In his cluttered office at police headquarters, Chief Carstairs sat alone, studying the clippings he had so meticulously cut from both the St. Louis *Post-Dispatch* and *Globe-Democrat*. Pearl Greenwood's dead face stared out at him from the front pages of the latest issues of both papers. At least the publishers could show only the head and not the mutilated body.

This murder was almost identical to the one the week before—the Daisy Dudler slashing. This time Captain Bernard had sent for the chief, insisting there was an obvious connection between the two killings. But matters seemed to have escalated—Pearl's body had been totally eviscerated, as if some unknown coroner had performed a careful autopsy. Someone using a very sharp straight razor or scalpel had removed all the organs and had neatly lined them up next to the body.

At the second bloody murder scene, Chief Carstairs had felt an eerie nagging that would not go away. It was as though this had all happened before. It had been as if he were reliving the crimes. Now, at his desk, it suddenly struck him—he had been reading about just such nightmarish slashings only recently.

The chief had been fascinated by the recent spate of senseless slashings in the Whitechapel section of London. He had been very disappointed when the killings stopped so abruptly, because the authorities had not yet caught

12

the killer. Whoever the madman was, and speculation abounded, it was obvious the mass murderer had called a sudden halt to his depredations.

But now the local papers screamed that Jack the Ripper had come to America and was menacing St. Louis! A cartoonist portrayed an evil creature clutching a straight razor dripping with blood—the Tower of London in the background. The thought had crossed Chief Carstairs's mind, but only briefly. There was a similarity, but it was impossible. The balding police chief rejected the idea as too simple, too improbable. Yet someone had performed ghoulish surgery on Daisy Dudler after she was dead, and someone had done a full postmortem on Pearl Greenwood. It looked as if the same person had wielded both knives.

A knock on the door brought the bulky police chief out of his thoughts. "Yes? Come on in."

"Sir, I did what you asked," Sergeant Laymon said, his ruddy complexion a little brighter than usual. "All the docs, vets, butchers, and barbers in town are being rounded up. But we ain't got room for 'em all here in our jail."

Dr. Louis Whitaker banged a fist on the bars of his cell and yelled at the guard: "Damn it, man! Do you know who I am! I happen to be one of the most reputable surgeons west of the Hudson! I am no common criminal, and I demand to see Chief Carstairs immediately! Someone has made a grave error, and by the time I'm finished with everyone responsible—" Indignation and rage blotched his reddened face. He sputtered and fumed, searching for words. "Do you have any idea whom you're dealing with here?"

"Y-yes, sir," the young guard said, putting as much "just following orders" into his reply as he could without turning and running.

"Then let me out of here!"

"Cain't, sir, 'Scuse me, sir!" He bolted from the room, clanging the door behind him.

Dr. Whitaker stared through the cell bars at the locked door and ignored the hoots of his fellow inmates. His heart thumped wildly in his chest. Taking a deep breath and then another, he automatically reached for his wrist with knowing fingers. His pulse was much too rapid, his blood pressure was going too high. The renowned surgeon knew he must calm himself or suffer the consequences. He wasn't a young man anymore, and if he didn't get a grip on his emotions, he wouldn't live to see fifty.

But this situation was insane. He had never been inside a jail before except to look at a patient once. Now he was being treated as if he were a common crook, with no reason given. Just because he had frequented Daisy every Wednesday night. That was no crime. But she was dead, brutally slashed, and he had nothing to do with that. He felt badly, but the murder had happened long after he had left her rooms. He had seen no one when he departed, and he was reasonably sure no one had seen him.

Of course, he thought, that might not be it at all. But what else could it be?

The door slammed open and a police officer dressed in street clothes strode in and stood in front of the surgeon's cell. "Dr. Whitaker, you are divorced, are you not?" No "Hello, how are you"—all business.

"What in hell does that have to do with anything?"

"Please, just answer my question."

Dr. Whitaker glared, but the policeman did not wither as he was intended to. The surgeon growled, "All right, yes. I am divorced from Priscilla—have been for nearly a year now. But how is that your business? What does my marital status have to do with my being here?"

Ignoring the question, the policeman continued, "Where

14

were you a week ago Wednesday evening—late, around one or two in the morning?''

''Who the hell are you to be asking me questions?''

Still all business, the young man replied, ''I am Captain Curtis Bernard, chief of detectives, sir. Now please answer the question. Where were you on—''

''I demand to see Chief Carstairs. Do you have any idea of how much trouble you are all in? You have the wrong man here!''

''Please answer my questions, Doctor, and you'll be out of here all the sooner.'' No emotional reaction. ''If you can't remember where you were a week ago Wednesday, where were you last—''

''How should I know! Wednesday-week, that's much too long ago! I keep a calendar of surgery and house calls, but not in the evening. I'm sure I was home in bed at that hour—where all decent people are.'' His gruffness receded.

Writing in a little notebook, the police captain kept his eyes on the page as he said, ''Do you have any witnesses, anyone who will swear you were home?''

''Are you impuning my word?'' Dr. Whitaker took a step toward Captain Bernard but realized his mistake. ''I'm certain my housekeeper will verify my whereabouts. But if she was also in bed asleep, as is every good citizen at that ungodly hour, she would not be able to say one way or the other. There was no one in my bed with me, I'm sorry to say—if it's any of your business.''

''Do you know a Daisy Dudler of Lafayette Avenue southeast?''

Dr. Whitaker realized his incarceration had something to do with her. But how could they possibly trace him to her? These primitive creatures were barking up the wrong tree.

''No,'' he said defiantly. ''Now I demand to see the police chief! Do you hear me?''

Pencil still poised, eyes still on the page, Captain Bernard cleared his throat dramatically and asked, "How about Pearl Greenwood?"

Dr. Whitaker stiffened as if he had been struck by a bolt of lightning. He turned his back and headed for the bunk. Looking at the floor, he sat heavily and refused to speak further. His silence filled the cell.

Captain Bernard shook his head as he went through the pages of his notebook with Chief Carstairs. "Except for Dr. Richard Lewis, who claims to have been away for a week and was on the stagecoach back from Hannibal when the first murder occurred, there's not a decent alibi among them. That Whitaker fellow is making the most noise—must have something to hide. When I asked him about the first victim, he didn't even stop to think before answering. Denied knowing her. If I were to guess, I'd say he did know her— professionally." He chuckled. "Hers, not his."

Chief Carstairs looked at him. "You might be right there. But did he know both women?"

"When I mentioned the second one, he went silent on me. Now he won't say a word—just sits there."

"He could simply be scared," the chief said, scratching his double chin, "or maybe he just likes tarts. Do we have enough to hold him on?"

Captain Bernard smiled. "No more than any of the others, Chief. Want to question him yourself?"

"Naw. Let's just let him cool his heels. If he thinks he's about to be charged, maybe he'll tell us what we want to know." Chief Carstairs lit his pipe and puffed. "Have the boys checked all the alibis yet?"

"There's too many suspects and not enough legmen, sir. And the public is getting upset." He pointed at the local headlines. "That isn't doing us any good, either."

Chief Carstairs slammed a beefy fist on the desk, causing the heavy kerosene lamp to jump. "Damn it, Curt, we're

16

trying everything. Two whores slit wide open, and the whole city's in an uproar. Husbands protecting wives, fathers watching over daughters.'' He shook his head and muttered almost to himself, ''With over a quarter of a million people in this city, I'm just afraid somebody may get hurt trying too hard to make their women safe.''

Clark Buttrick raised his voice to a bellow as he whipped his group into an angry mob. ''They gotta do something to keep that madman from slitting the throat of every woman in St. Louis!''

Cries of frustration overpowered his words. ''How?'' ''What do we do?'' ''Let's do something!'' There was lynching in their eyes, but they had no villain to hang yet.

Buttrick howled over the mob, ''Let's tell old woman Carstairs! If he don't do somethin' quick, he'd better take a hike! We'll hunt down that yellow critter for him.''

More shouts, angrier and louder. ''Yeah, let's hunt the bastard down!'' ''Let's get the varmint!'' ''Find the slasher!'' ''Kill him!'' ''Hangin's too good for 'im!''

''Follow me, boys!'' the husky leader shouted, starting off down the street toward police headquarters. Striding forcefully, enjoying the surge of power as the group stayed close behind, Buttrick glanced back first to the right and then to the left, assuring his followers as they went. They were a lynch mob without a rope, but this was merely a warning. He would let the St. Louis Police Department know he was in charge here and was a force to reckon with. This would teach the police to respect him instead of constantly harassing him.

Sergeant Laymon bounced into the chief's office before Chief Carstairs could answer his short knock. ''Joe Hobbs got us a witness, sir!'' the sergeant said, barely able to conceal his excitement.

Chief Carstairs put down his pipe and waited as Sergeant Laymon stepped aside. The chief knew better than to get his hopes up, but he was under pressure from vigilante and church groups, as well as the mayor. Something had to be done fast to find and stop the slasher. Could this be the break in the case he had been looking for?

Sergeant Hobbs popped his scraggly head through the doorway, a big grin displaying two teeth missing. "Chief!" he said in greeting, "I got somebody here fer you to meet." Beckoning to someone outside the door, he said, "This here is Tillie Jenkins, sir." He called out, "Come on in, Tillie. It's all right, darlin'."

A plump child peered cautiously around the doorway, her wide eyes nearly popping at the sight of the huge police chief. She shuffled her feet and glanced from Sergeant Hobbs to Sergeant Laymon to Chief Carstairs, twirling at her skirt until the rough-woven material nearly ripped.

Nodding beneficently, Chief Carstairs winked at Sergeant Laymon and said, "Thank you, Dickie."

The sergeant understood and took his cue to leave quietly without disturbing the young witness.

The chief remained seated so as not to scare the girl, smiled disarmingly, and said, "My, such a lovely young lady. How old are you, Tillie?"

Sergeant Hobbs nodded. "She's going on ten, sir. But she's a good girl and a good worker. Her mum told me how she takes care of all the little ones—seven of 'em—while the older kids work on the docks."

Tillie beamed and dug her toe into an imaginary rug.

"Well, Tillie, where do you live?" Chief Carstairs asked, attempting to break the ice.

"Two-fourteen Lafayette southeast, sir." She looked at Sergeant Hobbs and tugged at a long chestnut braid.

"Go on, Tillie, dear. Tell Chief Carstairs what you know about poor Miss Dudler—Daisy. It's all right; we're all friends here. You wanna help us, don't you?'' Sergeant Hobbs smiled warmly.

The chief knew Sergeant Hobbs's six children and how well he dealt with them. If anyone could get Tillie to talk, Hobbs could. He waited patiently for Sergeant Hobbs to coax the youngster.

The sergeant reached into his uniform pocket and withdrew a lump of something wrapped in waxed paper. Offering it to the girl, he said, "Your throat must be dry. Here, this taffy my daughter Phoebe made should help.''

Tillie took the piece of candy, unwrapped it, and popped it into her mouth. With the lump firmly wedged into her cheek, she said, "I miss Daisy.'' Her eyes clouded up as she looked from Sergeant Hobbs to Chief Carstairs and back.

"Yes, I'm sure you do,'' the chief said.

"She was real nice to me—she let me wear her lip rouge and play dress-up in her gowns and furs and jewelry.'' Her voice trailed off as her shyness returned. She pulled at her braid and snuffled.

Sergeant Hobbs said, "Sir, when I questioned her, Tillie told me she used to go to Daisy's room whenever she could after she finished her chores around the house. She lives right across the street from Daisy's and spent a good amount of time there.''

Tillie added sadly, "Daisy was so nice.''

Chief Carstairs nodded at Sergeant Hobbs and smiled at the young girl. "Of course she was.''

"Daisy told Tillie all about her steady Wednesday gentleman—the surgeon—how happy she was with him. Told her he was a very rich man''—Hobbs glanced at the girl—"right, Tillie?'' She nodded. "He gave Daisy expensive gifts and money. Daisy confided to Tillie that she really loved the man and hoped that he might even marry her.''

Tillie sighed and wound her braid around her finger.

The sergeant continued: "Daisy claimed that the surgeon

19

left his wife for her, but that he had to wait before he could marry her. There was no actual proposal of marriage, just hope and speculation on Daisy's part, from what I gather."

Tillie's bright eyes clouded again. "Now I'll never know." The young girl began to lose her composure.

Sergeant Hobbs came to her side and put his big fleshy arm around her, comforting her. "Now, don't you cry, li'l darlin'. It's all right." He handed her his handkerchief.

She took the candy from her mouth and put it in her pocket, then blew her nose heartily, handing the sergeant back a soggy piece of cloth.

Chief Carstairs took this opportunity to ask a question. "Did you ever meet this Wednesday gentleman of Daisy's?"

Tillie's face brightened. "Oh, yes! He's ever so handsome. And so nice. He'd never hurt Daisy." She frowned and said defiantly, "And he'd never kill her!"

"When was the last time you saw him, Tillie?" the chief asked conversationally.

She stared at the ceiling for a moment, her tongue licking residue of the taffy from her lips. She squinted at the wall, trying very hard to remember the exact moment she had last seen him. Finally she said, "I don't remember. Maybe a week ago. I don't know."

The chief asked, "Where did you see him—at Daisy's?"

She shook her head. "Out front. He was coming to see her like always." She lowered her voice to a near-whisper as she confided, "He's got a fancy carriage."

Sergeant Hobbs broke in. "Tillie told me he always got out at the corner of Lafayette and Broadway and walked to Third. Never rode right up to the door."

"Do you remember what he looks like?" the chief asked, beginning a casual interrogation.

"Of course I do." She giggled.

"Could you tell us?"

"He's very, very handsome."

"How tall?"

"Big—much bigger'n Sergeant Hobbs."

"What color are his eyes and hair?"

She thought for a moment. "Kind of greenish-brown—his eyes." She giggled and twirled her braid.

"His hair? Dark, light, lots, bald?"

She frowned. "Brown, with silver in it. And a grand mustache."

"How old is he?"

She looked at the two men blankly and shrugged her shoulders. "'Bout as old as my dad."

"How old is your father?" Chief Carstairs asked.

"How should I know?"

Sergeant Hobbs winked at the chief. "Brad Jenkins is about forty, sir, give or take a year or two."

"Would you know Daisy's Wednesday gentleman if you saw him again?" Chief Carstairs asked as if testing her.

"Of course I would!" she rose to the challenge. "Why, I'd know Dr. Whitaker anywhere!"

Chapter 3

Jessica Starbuck stared at the lengthy telegram, reading it a second time. As she handed it across the low mahogany table to Ki, she said, "There's more than just coincidence here." Her voice echoed in the vastness of the Starbuck mansion main salon, and she leaned a little more toward the blazing logs in the massive marble fireplace.

The Japanese-American put aside the Fort Worth *Chronicle*, turned up the kerosene lamp on the table next to him, and slowly plodded through the wire, nodding as he read. When he finished, he looked up, his dark almond eyes locking onto Jessie's.

"I see what you mean," he said quietly, looking back at the local newspaper beside him on the brocade-covered chesterfield. "Yes, there's definitely some connection between the two."

Jessie's large green eyes flashed as she glanced from the telegram to the newspaper. "First we read a front-page story here in Texas telling us that London's Jack the Ripper is massacring half the women of St. Louis, and then we get a telegram from one of Father's oldest school chums asking for help because the police and the vigilante groups believe he's the culprit."

She took the telegram from Ki and scanned it once more. "Pure insanity! The whole idea of a man of Dr. Whitaker's professional stature being suspected of such bloodthirsty crimes is completely crazy." She hesitated a moment, considering all sides of her argument. "Of course, I never actually met the man," she said in all honesty. "But Father spoke fondly of him often."

Ki said, "Professional standing and a soft spot in your father's heart for someone do not guarantee the man's innocence. You know that." He frowned. "And I'm sure you noticed that Dr. Whitaker's telegram is addressed to *Alex* Starbuck; so the surgeon is not only unaware of your father's death, but obviously has not contacted him in years. People can change a good deal over time."

"You're right, but something in his plea rings true." She smiled. "Besides, I just received a letter from one of my dearest friends, Joy Madison, the famous actress. In her letter she says the play she's touring in is about to open in St. Louis. She's invited us to her opening night, but her letter arrived too late. The show opened yesterday." Jessica's voice took on an air of excitement as she continued, "I haven't seen Joy in a play since college days. St. Louis is the farthest west she has ever been, and she's starring in a melodrama on a permanently moored riverboat!"

Ki stood. "I'll be ready to travel within the hour. When you're packed, we'll leave."

"I'd rather we take the train. St. Louis is a long way off, and we're going to need our city clothes. We should be prepared for just about anything."

Ki smiled. Then he stopped and turned. "I'll arrange for passage on the next train north. Do you want to wire Dr. Whitaker yourself, or shall I?"

"No, thank you. I'd appreciate it if you took care of that, too." As an afterthought, she jotted down something on a scrap of paper and handed it to Ki. "Here, I would also appreciate it if you sent this message to Joy Madison at her theater telling her we're on our way and should be in town next week. Tell her I'll contact her as soon as we arrive to

24

let her know where we're staying.'' She paused and smiled. ''And don't mention my father to Dr. Whitaker. Just tell him that help is on the way.''

As Jessica and Ki alighted from the train in St. Louis at the brand-new Union Station's Grand Hall, all eyes turned to watch the honey-blonde. Her firm breasts fit tightly inside her yellow silk blouse, barely covered by a small leather vest, and her form-fitting leather traveling skirt emphasized her shapely hips and narrow waistline. Just a flash of flesh showed between fringed skirt hem and matching boots as she stepped from the train, but it was enough to stop foot traffic in all directions.

Ki smiled to himself, observing the expected reaction to the beauty he had sworn to protect. Few eyes strayed toward him, and he was sure that those who did see him, even with St. Louis's own broad blend of French, German, Italian, and Spanish citizens, would take him for an Indian—some people did. His long black hair held in place by a braided leather thong added to his quiet mystique.

Jessica had already inquired about the best hotel in town, which was conveniently located near the train station. Ki had a porter carry their luggage to the splendid hotel lobby, and Jessica checked in for both of them, requesting a suite with connecting bedrooms. The desk clerk hesitated until he saw the Starbuck name on the register—the Starbuck empire was well known even this far northeast. He assigned them the hotel's finest suite.

As she waited for the hotel porter to collect their luggage, Jessie wrote a note on a piece of hotel stationery and asked the desk clerk to have it delivered to Joy Madison's theater. She would see her friend as soon as she and Ki had been to the police station to meet with Dr. Whitaker.

After bathing away their travel dust, and changing into city clothes, Ki and Jessie had the hotel doorman hail a

25

taxicab to take them to police headquarters, just a few blocks away. When they arrived, they asked to see Dr. Whitaker and were told to wait. In a matter of minutes Captain Bernard appeared and introduced himself.

"Captain Curtis Bernard, ma'am, chief of detectives. You want to see Dr. Louis Whitaker? How do you know him?" The police captain openly admired Jessie and all but ignored Ki. He noted that the color of the silk gown under her dark-green cape matched her lime-green eyes. Her beauty enchanted and unsettled him, and he wondered what her relationship to the Chinaman was. More than likely, he was a servant.

Jessica stared into the policeman's soft crystal-blue eyes and replied, "Dr. Whitaker is an old friend of the family." Was there a hint of a blush in her cheeks? The police officer's ruggedness showed through his suit as she wondered how he would look in jeans.

Ki said, "Miss Starbuck is the daughter of the late Alex Starbuck of the Lone Star empire. Louis Whitaker and her father went to school together."

Jessie took in the police captain's interesting face, light curly hair, and appealing physique and noted the instant body chemistry. She smiled brightly and continued, "I'd appreciate it very much, Captain, if my associate and I could see Dr. Whitaker as soon as possible. We're visiting from Texas."

Associate? What kind of associate? Captain Bernard wondered. "Follow me." He led the way down one barren corridor after another, then stopped at a battered old desk and spoke in hushed tones to the uniformed guard seated behind the desk.

The guard nodded, looked past his superior to the guests, and stood.

"Mullins here will see you to the surgeon's cell," Captain

26

Bernard said as he headed back in the direction they had just come. "Ma'am . . . sir." He nodded to Jessie and Ki and left, his heavy boots echoing along the hallway.

Officer Mullins took charge. "You'll have to leave any weapons out here." He looked from Jessica to Ki, not expecting either of them to be bearing arms.

Jessica smiled daintily and shrugged. The derringer in her little handbag would remain out of sight.

Ki raised his arms to prove he wore no gun. He was sure the policeman had never seen a *shuriken* and would never consider the sharp throwing star a weapon.

Satisfied, Officer Mullins picked up a heavy ring of keys and searched through them. Unlocking the massive metal door to the cells, he gestured for the visitors to enter. He led Jessie and Ki past several foul-smelling drunks and disreputable-looking characters to a far cell that held a slender, distinguished-appearing man.

"Hey, Doc, you got visitors!" Mullins called out. Turning to Jessie, the guard said, "Take as long as you want—he ain't goin' nowhere." He snorted as he laughed at his own joke.

"Thank you," Jessie said sweetly, waiting until the guard was out of earshot before speaking. When she heard the metal door being locked, she said, "Dr. Whitaker, I am Jessica Starbuck, Alex's daughter. I'm sorry to report that my father has been dead now for quite some time—murdered."

Whitaker rose from his cot and approached the bars of the cell. He stared from Jessie to Ki and back again, saying nothing. He looked defeated.

Ignoring the surgeon's dejection, Jessie continued: "This is Ki, my father's most trusted friend and companion, and now mine. We came as soon as we could. Please try to tell us what's going on."

Dr. Whitaker explained the series of events that had led

to his incarceration. He had been held without bail for what seemed like weeks, and even his ex-wife's pleadings had not stirred the hearts of those in charge. He was guilty of no more than frequenting ladies of the evening—and now two of the women he had been seeing were brutally slashed to death.

"There's nothing wrong with seeing one of those women," he said defensively, tugging at his mustache, "although my ex-wife, Priscilla, would debate that. In fact, my seeing prostitutes contributed immeasurably to the ultimate failure of my marriage." He looked down in what Jessica could only take to be embarrassment. "I don't know how she found out, but she did. Whenever I visited one, Priscilla would fly into an unreasoning rage." He avoided Jessie's gaze, speaking to Ki, as if a man might better understand.

Ki nodded. "Go on," he said.

Jessica, sensing the surgeon's uneasiness, looked away to reduce his discomfort. She opened her handbag and rummaged through it to break eye contact.

"My visits to those young women meant nothing to me—nothing more than a little change of pace, a dalliance pure and simple. But when Priscilla turned cold, I was forced to seek my—" He broke off, unable to say anything more in front of Jessica, and pulled at his mustache.

"Please, Dr. Whitaker, I understand fully. Then what happened?"

"Priscilla's jealousy grew so unreasoning that I finally left her. Our marriage had become one long argument interrupted by violent tantrums. She had been such a brilliant young woman, and I turned her into a shrew."

Jessica and Ki looked on sympathetically as the surgeon continued.

"We had had no children, although God knows we had tried. Poor Priscilla—she'd miscarried twice. Blamed her-

28

self for our inability to have children." He shook his head sadly. "She's such a perfectionist." His thoughts appeared to drift momentarily as he stared into space, twisting his mustache.

Jessie pulled him back to the present. "Do the police know about your connection with either of the two murdered girls?"

"Somehow, they seem to have found out that I visited both Daisy and Pearl." He explained his arrangement with the two women. "The police cannot be certain of the time, but they know I had been frequenting both on a regular basis. One at a time, of course."

The surgeon took out a silk handkerchief and daubed his upper lip just below the mustache. "I'm not sure if they know that I saw each just a few hours before her demise." His voice sounded strained as he continued. "In fact, the thought crossed my mind that had I stayed but just a short while longer, each would be alive today."

Ki shook his head emphatically. "Doctor, don't take responsibility for these tragedies. How do you know that if you had stayed longer, you might not also have been a victim of the murderous slasher?"

Dr. Whitaker stared at the Asian, his mind obviously racing. Jessica could see that such a concept had never occurred to the surgeon. He had been wallowing in remorse, guilt, and self-pity without any idea of the danger he might have been in.

Jessie smiled. "Please don't worry. We're going to arrange for bail to be set. Once you're out of this oppressive environment, you might start thinking more clearly. We will do everything we can to solve this case and clear your name."

Dr. Whitaker looked Jessie up and down, shook his head gravely, and said, "I cannot ask you to become involved in this mess. When I asked for assistance, I expected my

29

old friend Alex to come to my rescue, as he often did when we were in school.'' His wry smirk betrayed his thoughts as he glanced at Ki's lack of weapons and Jessica's apparent fragility. ''But a lovely young woman and an unarmed Oriental? My intention is to be neither rude nor ungrateful, but what could you possibly—''

Ki interrupted before Jessie could speak. ''Please, Dr. Whitaker, do not allow appearances to fool you. Both of us are quite capable of assisting you. We would not have traveled all the way from Texas had we not believed this to be true.''

''Yes,'' Jessica shot in, ''it's what we do since Father's murder—and Father would be pleased that we had the opportunity to come to your aid.''

Chapter 4

Chief Carstairs stood firm as he faced Jessica and Ki. His ruddy complexion darkened as he spoke. "There can be no bail for Dr. Whitaker!" he growled. "Two slashings, performed by someone well acquainted with surgerical procedures, call for drastic measures. Dr. Whitaker is a surgeon, he knew both the victims, and he was seen going into or leaving both victims' rooms on the night of each murder. We have witnesses, you know! What more need I say?"

The police chief pulled hard at his collar, and the button came loose as the celluloid sprang up. He shoved it back down, but it refused to stay down, so he finally yanked the collar off and threw it onto his desk. Agitated, he grabbed a pipe from its rack and tamped some fresh tobacco into the blackened bowl with his thumb.

Jessica opened her mouth to speak, but stopped. The chief was preoccupied with trying to find a match, rummaging in one drawer after another, then in one pocket after another. She waited until he finally found a match in his vest pocket and lighted his pipe.

Finally she began, "Chief, if I may—"

"No, you may not." He puffed deeply, resembling an overstuffed dragon. "There will be no bail, young lady, and that is that!"

Ki tried to weaken the police chief's resolve, saying,

31

"We want no favors, Chief, merely justice. Are you declaring Dr. Whitaker guilty without benefit of trial? Is that how you do things in St. Louis?"

Jessica chimed in, "If bail were to be set, how much would it be?"

Chief Carstairs looked amused. The young woman had unwittingly provided him with a means of stopping these pests cold. Smugly he said, "I've changed my mind. I will speak to the judge about setting bail."

"Right away?" Jessie asked impatiently.

"Of course. We wouldn't want it to be said that justice was not served here in St. Louis. Follow me."

The police chief led Jessica and Ki to the far end of the building and stopped before a door marked JUDGE HASTINGS. He knocked and let himself in, saying, "Wait here."

Jessie and Ki smiled at each other and stood there in the hall, knowing fully what to expect.

Moments later Chief Carstairs stepped back into the corridor, beaming broadly. "All right, folks, the judge has set bail. If you want to post bond for Dr. Whitaker, just see the clerk at the front desk," he said, pointing down the hall toward the entrance to the building. "But I must warn you, we only take cash—no checks."

His hearty laugh bounced off the corridor walls as he lumbered off in the opposite direction, a thick trail of smoke flowing in his wake. He called back over his shoulder, "By the way, folks, bail's one hundred thousand dollars."

There was a chill in the air as evening approached. The sun dipped below the horizon, and Jessie and Ki hurried down Market Street. After a brief visit to a local bank, where Jessica presented a letter of unlimited credit from the Circle Star Ranch account in Fort Worth, she and Ki returned in the growing dusk to police headquarters. A bank executive accompanied them, lugging a big satchel filled with large bills. He would verify the bag's contents. Plunking the satchel down in front of the desk sergeant, they requested Dr. Whitaker's release on bail.

The desk sergeant sent Chief Carstairs a note asking about bail and received an immediate response. As he read the reply from the chief, all could hear the booming laughter coming from the police chief's office.

"One hundred thousand dollars!" the stunned policeman kept repeating, unable to believe his eyes.

"It's all there," stammered the fragile bank manager, confused by the transaction and wanting to get home to his wife's pot roast. He timidly opened the satchel for the policeman to see inside.

After verifying the bag's contents, the desk sergeant sent for Dr. Whitaker, signed a receipt for the hundred thousand dollars, and released the surgeon on bail.

Half an hour later a roar thundered from Chief Carstairs's office. "They did *what*?!"

Clark Buttrick flung a chair clear across the room and yelled, "Dammit all to blue blazes! They cain't dismiss me that easily! Them cusses don't know who they're dealin' with here! I'll make them sorry bastards curse the day they ever crossed me!"

The husky man's massive neck went from ears to shoulders, and colored a bright pink as he boomed, the thick veins standing out and pulsing visibly. Great drops of sweat sat on his high receding forehead and rolled down his cheeks, matting his dirty blond hair. His beady gray eyes narrowed, and his lipless mouth contorted in drunken anger. He threw his head back and took a long swig of red-eye from the bottle, then wiped his mouth with the back of his hairy hand.

"Dammit all to blue blazes!" he muttered, splashing red-eye down the thick blond hair on his arm and onto his equally hairy chest.

His fat wife, Fanny, cowered in a corner of the front room and hoped her sodden husband's tantrum would wane soon. But she knew that when her husband got this liquored up, she could do very little to stop him. Her only salvation would come if he passed out. She brushed thin wisps of hair from her eyes, tried to remain as quiet and inconspicuous as she could, and watched her husband intently.

"I'll fix them, I will. They ain't gonna make no fool out of me!" Buttrick slammed a heavily booted foot into the side of the broken-down chesterfield, lifting it up off the floor.

Startled, Fanny yelped.

He wheeled on her. "So you're against me, too, are you, Fanny!"

He made a lunge for her, but she anticipated his move. She grabbed the kerosene lamp and scooted off to the bedroom, bolting and barring the door from inside. He could bang all he wanted, but the door was sturdy—hadn't he built it himself to protect them from intruders? All the cursing in the world was not going to bring that door down, and Fanny knew her husband's anger would subside as the whiskey wore off.

In disgust the heavyset woman plopped herself down on the edge of the bed, rolls of fat hanging over, and waited. She knew better than to come out before her husband had slept off his drunken rage. But as she sat there listening, she heard something that bothered her—silence. Something was wrong. This was not part of her husband's usual pattern. By now, with her safely barricaded behind the stout wooden door, Clark would have demolished almost every stick of furniture, every plate and cup and piece of pottery in the rest of the house.

Fanny knew this and was accustomed to it. That was why

34

she kept her most precious possessions in the bedroom, out of harm's way, and that was why she would always grab the lamp and run. Someday he might knock it over and burn the place down. This way he had only the light of the fireplace to see by. Gradually Clark's whiskey storm would diminish, and it would be safe for her to unbar the door and try to salvage some of the destruction.

Silence meant even more danger. She strained to hear something, anything—his heavy breathing, his boots shuffling on the bare floor—something. But there was nothing—nothing but the loud thumping of her heart, the pounding in her temples throbbing in her ears. She pressed herself to the door, but she knew it was too thick to allow her to hear soft sounds. She sniffed at the door jamb, but she smelled no smoke. Fear mounted as she leaned against the wall and tried to hear through it. The silence hurt her ears, it was so deafening. Her double chins wobbled as she tried to calm herself, but panic welled up within her breast as she thought the very worst.

Clark must be dead—his heart had surely given out. She had always worried that his rages would be the death of him. It never seemed natural for someone's face to turn deep purple, the way his always did at the peak of his tantrums, without causing harm to his body. And if he were dead, who would support her and the children? Of course, all eight of the kids worked, bringing in small wages from the brewery and the docks. But she knew she could not exist without her Clark. Not without her husband.

With a cry of terror, the obese woman yanked the bar off the door and rushed from her hiding place. She trundled from room to room, searching through debris for her husband's body, but it wasn't there. She realized he was no longer in the house. He had gone out into the deepening dusk in his fury. Her entire body relaxed a degree from relief. At least he was not dead.

35

As she picked up bits of furniture and broken plates and bottles, her gaze fell above the rickety mantelpiece—the empty mantelpiece where Clark's Winchester always hung. Three large nails protruded where the weapon had been, and a lighter patch of wall showed an outline of the rifle on the grimy paint.

Fanny's mind raced—should she run after him and try to stop him from harming someone or himself? But where had he gone? Had he headed for city hall to kill the mayor, or to police headquarters to do in Chief Carstairs, or had he just gone off to shoot up the town? The sun had already set, and darkness had enveloped the pathetic row houses. She knew it would not be safe out there for a lone woman, even one of her immense size. The wife of Clark Buttrick, leader of the vigilantes against the mad slasher, should know that better than anyone.

After straightening up the house as much as possible, and putting away what hadn't been broken, Fanny Buttrick seated herself at the kitchen table. By the light of a kerosene lamp, she emptied the cookie jar, then the bread box, then the cupboards and the larder, compulsively eating herself into a near-stupor.

Jessica and Ki returned to the hotel after arranging bail. They suggested Dr. Whitaker come with them, but he insisted on going home first to bathe and change his clothes. His request seemed reasonable enough, so they agreed to meet him in their hotel lobby at seven for a drink before dinner. Both Jessie and Ki noticed the plainclothes policeman who was apparently following the surgeon. That was exactly what they hoped the police would do. In that way, if anything further were to happen, should there be any more murders, Dr. Whitaker would have a foolproof alibi.

When Ki asked the desk clerk for their key, he was handed a note addressed to Jessica Starbuck. In it, Jessie read, Joy

Madison would be pleased to see her any time. The play was only performed on weekends, so her weekdays were free. She was staying at a theatrical rooming house near Eads Bridge, but her rooms had a back entrance for privacy. She was disappointed that Jessie had not been able to be at her opening, but she looked forward to seeing her the following day. Jessie sent an immediate reply that she would see Joy the next morning at ten.

On the dot of seven that evening Dr. Whitaker strode through the front entrance to the hotel, the unobtrusive policeman close on his trail. Jessica noted how dapper the surgeon appeared, freshly shaved and in his evening garb.

The surgeon smiled broadly. "You are quite beautiful in that shade of blue, Miss Starbuck. Alex would be extremely proud of you. You have the best of your mother and your father, both."

Ki smiled his agreement.

Lowering her long lashes, Jessica thanked the surgeon and suggested a drink before dinner. As Dr. Whitaker called for a waiter, Jessica whispered something to Ki, who excused himself and sauntered over to the plainclothes policeman assigned to follow the surgeon.

"Pardon me, sir," Ki said quietly, "but if you are not otherwise occupied, would you care to join my friends and me for a drink and dinner?" When the surprised policeman frowned and shook his head, Ki continued. "It would be far simpler to keep an eye on Dr. Whitaker if you were part of our party, don't you agree?"

The plainclothesman at first denied his role, but finally concluding it was no use, he acquiesced and followed Ki back to the table.

"You may call me Ki," the tall Asian said with great dignity. Turning to the others, he said, "Jessica Starbuck, Dr. Whitaker, this is—" Ki waited for the man to introduce himself.

"Uh, the name's Detective Jeggi, sir, ma'am. John Jeggi. That's spelled with a *J* but pronounced with a *Y*—Scandinavian, you know."

The policeman looked uncomfortably from face to face and brushed a wild lock of dark brown hair from his eyes. "I should not be doing this, but this feller here, uh, Ki, made a good point. As long as you know I'm assigned to you, I might as well stay with you." He tugged at his collar, coughed to clear his throat, and glanced around uneasily.

"What would you like to drink, detective?" Ki asked as the waiter came to take their order.

"I shouldn't have nothing—on duty, you know." He looked around the room again. "Oh, well, if you insist— four fingers of red-eye, if you please."

The waiter smiled. "We have rye, bourbon, or Scotch whiskey—no red-eye, sir."

"Scotch, then," Detective Jeggi said uncomfortably.

After drinks the four adjourned to the hotel restaurant for a gourmet meal. The policeman prattled on as each ensuing glass of Scotch loosened his tongue a bit more. He refused the brandy to top off the meal, preferring just one more shot of Scotch to go with his cigar.

Jessica, Ki, and Dr. Whitaker agreed to meet the following morning to plan their strategy for proving the surgeon's innocence, and Dr. Whitaker called for his carriage as Detective Jeggi stood by uneasily.

When the ornate vehicle finally reached its destination inside the elegant walled-in Vandeventer Place section of the city, the surgeon invited Detective Jeggi to continue his surveillance from within, where it was warm and comfortable. After first adamantly refusing, the soggy plainclothesman eyed the huge stone mansion and gave in, accepting with gratitude the surgeon's thoughtful hospitality. He rationalized that no one would know, and he could definitely watch the surgeon better from inside.

Entering a small den off the cavernous main hallway, the two men sat in front of a toasty fire the housekeeper had laid for the surgeon. They lit cigars and drank another shot or two from a crystal decanter, chatting about nothing in particular and purposely avoiding any mention of the murders. Then Dr. Whitaker assured Detective Jeggi that from his seat in the den he could look out on the staircase—the only way to or from the bedrooms.

The surgeon bade the police detective a gracious good night and went upstairs to bed, leaving the plainclothesman to warm himself by the fire as he sipped an excellent Scotch whiskey from the decanter.

The young woman's long blond ringlets bounced as she walked quickly down the street. A cabbie reined in his horse and called out flirtatiously, but the woman looked straight ahead, her thoughts far away. She tugged closely at the full-length tweed cape and tried to keep the hood up, but it kept slipping off her masses of curls. The dampness of the cold air off the Mississippi River chilled her to the bone; she was accustomed to a much drier cold. Only one more block, just around the corner, and she would be in the warmth of her rooms.

To the few passersby on Washington Avenue so late that evening, the young woman appeared to be talking to herself. As the fog horns moaned off the river and the clatter of hooves echoed down the cobblestones, she mumbled something, intent on getting out of the cold night air as soon as possible. One well-dressed young couple, scurrying to hail a taxicab, glanced her way and tittered cruelly. A drunk, stinking of cheap wine and vomit, lurched at her, nearly knocking her off her footing. She quickened her pace and broke into a near-trot, blond curls bobbing.

Returning to her rooms by herself had been a ill-conceived idea, she reflected as she tried to avoid dark shadows and any further tosspots. She should have accepted a ride or a companion to walk her back. One could never be too careful, especially after those murders.

"May I escort you home, my dear?" came a husky voice from behind.

"Thank you, no," she said emphatically and kept up her brisk stride.

Another drunk headed toward her, lunging for her handbag. He grabbed her cloak instead and nearly wrenched it off her. The frantic young woman tugged it free and hurried on, wishing herself already home.

The voice from behind came closer, now at her elbow, gentle, insistent. "At least permit me to see you safely to your rooms. It is not prudent for a lovely young lady to be out at this hour, you know."

There was something cultured in the voice, something very understanding. She looked at the expensive overcoat, muffler, and hat. There was no odor of liquor. As she kept walking, she momentarily looked up into the shadowy face and smiled, her garish makeup making a mockery of her young good looks. Yes, perhaps an escort would be a good idea, she reasoned. There was less than a block to go, and someone to fend off drunks and cabbies would make the warmth and safety of her rooms all that much closer.

"Thank you," she said without missing a step. She extended her arm and hooked it around the well-dressed stranger's proffered elbow. "Are you on your way to visit a patient?" she asked, glancing down at the little black physician's satchel.

"You might say that," came the reply. "I do have an appointment of sorts. And in your direction."

"What luck. To be quite candid, your company is most welcome." The distant lamplight cast an eerie shadow on her exaggerated rouge. "From what I've been reading in the newspapers, I'm taking a chance on the streets."

The strong arm entwined with hers squeezed her reassuringly. "Yes, my dear, this is your lucky night."

The tiny young woman smiled. "We're almost there— it's right over there." She pointed across the street.

When they came to the front gate, she stopped and patted her escort's hand as she withdrew her arm. "This is it. Be it ever so humble—" She laughed. "Thank you so much. You'll never know just how much I appreciate your company."

"You're not home yet, my dear. Please allow me to walk you to your door."

"That's really not necessary. If you'll be kind enough to watch me from the gate, here, I'll be fine."

A gloved hand took her by the arm and led her through the gate. "I insist. The least I can do is see you safely to your door."

"All right." She rummaged in her overfilled handbag and brought out a large latchkey. "I use the private entrance in the back."

The two carefully felt their way along the path to the back of the building and up a flight of stairs. At the door she extended a hand to thank her escort once again.

"Open it—let's make sure it's safe. I won't feel I've done my duty till I see you safely inside."

She opened the door and stepped in to turn on the lamp. She laughed. "No mad ripper in here."

She turned and saw three coins extended in the palm of the gloved hand. She laughed again, shaking her head, her blond curls swaying.

"Sorry, mister, if I gave you the wrong impression. I may look easy, but please believe me—I'm not. Please leave, and thank you again."

"You want more?"

"What I want is for you to leave now."

"No, I want to buy your services. Do you think you're too good for me, is that it?"

"You're making a mistake. Please leave before I call for the landlady." She headed for the door to the roominghouse hallway. "In fact, I'm going to call for her now. She'll get the police. You wouldn't want that, now, would you?"

She grabbed the doorknob and twisted it. Locked. Then she remembered that the key to the hallway was on the dresser. As she rushed to the bureau, she heard the clasps of the little black satchel snap open. She grabbed the key and dashed for the door. From the corner of her eye, she could see her intruder.

What's he doing?! Oh, my God! He's taking off his clothes!

★

Chapter 5

Glaring sunlight poured in on Detective Jeggi's soundly sleeping form. He shifted positions in the plush wingback chair, yelped in pain, and sat upright with a start. He had not planned on falling asleep—he was on duty and should have kept watch over the staircase. But those last few glasses of Scotch whiskey must have been his ruination. He tried to jump to his feet, but his body resisted the command. Instead, he slowly eased himself forward and upward, finally standing, one leg resting against the chair for support, his limbs crying out in agony.

"Sleep well?" came a chipper voice from the hallway.

Detective Jeggi turned to see Dr. Whitaker grinning at him, rubbing his hands in apparent anticipation. The plainclothesman's vision blurred momentarily, and he squinted and made an attempt to speak, but nothing came out. He cleared his throat painfully and gulped. He stroked his throat and felt the day-old stubble. In sharp contrast he noted that the surgeon had bathed, shaved, and changed into morning clothes.

Ignoring the police detective's obvious discomfort, Dr. Whitaker asked, "Ready for breakfast?" Without waiting for a reply, he motioned for the plainclothesman to follow him into the dinning room, where the housekeeper had put out a sumptuous hot buffet.

Detective Jeggi's stomach lurched as he surveyed the

43

scrambled eggs, sizzling steak, fried bread, and French breakfast pastries. Steam rose from the sterling silver coffee and tea service, and the aromas calmed his insides. Without being asked, he headed for the coffee and poured himself a cup of scalding liquid.

"What a beautiful day!" Dr. Whitaker commented as he heaped his plate with food. "I could eat an elephant!" Sitting at the head of the long carved-oak table, he began to demolish the serving. Between sips of coffee, he ate as if starved. The surgeon returned for another ample helping as the police detective watched in amazement.

"You always eat like that?" Detective Jeggi asked, unable to control his curiosity.

"For someone as thin and wiry as I am," the surgeon replied, chuckling, "I seem to require more fuel than most. It is a small wonder that I have not the gigantic abdomen most men display at my age and with my appetite."

Detective Jeggi nodded and reached for a breakfast roll. Dipping it into his coffee, he sucked the liquid from it before cramming it into his mouth. As he munched, he withdrew his watch from his pocket and stared at it, trying in vain to compute the time. He regretted his mind was still not fully functional.

Dr. Whitaker glanced at the porcelain-and-gilt eight-day clock on the sideboard. "Just minutes before eight. We should be on our way as soon as possible if we are to be on time to meet Miss Starbuck and her associate."

"Yeah, that's right." The plainclothesman poured himself another cup of coffee and stuffed down another soggy piece of pastry. His eyes began to clear, and he felt almost human again. He just might live, after all.

While Detective Jeggi poured himself a third cup of coffee and reached for yet another breakfast roll, Dr. Whitaker summoned the housekeeper and asked for his carriage to be brought around.

44

The plainclothesman followed the surgeon out the front door, carelessly dropping crumbs as he chomped down the last of the pastry. He was oblivious to the housekeeper's furious glare as she scurried to snatch each crumb from the priceless Persian rug before it could cause permanent damage.

As the elaborate carriage carried them through the elaborate stone Vandeventer Place gate, Detective Jeggi realized how grand the area was. By daylight the immense expanse of ponderous acreage surrounding each mansion made this exclusive section of the city all the more impressive. The famous surgeon's splendid attire seemed all the more grand in the bright sunlight, especially when compared to his own humble, rumpled clothing.

It slowly dawned on the police detective how unbelievably wealthy the surgeon must be.

In the drawing room of their suite, Jessica and Ki enjoyed a fine leisurely breakfast of Louisiana French cuisine. They both found it a little difficult, however, to swallow the chicory-laced coffee, something neither had been able to acquire a taste for on their trips to New Orleans. It was apparent that the hotel's chef had been influenced by this singularly Southern touch.

In the hotel lobby just before eight o'clock, Jessica asked the desk clerk about the play that had recently opened at the Floating Palace. He reported that the critics had raved about the young leading lady—the melodrama was a huge success and should stay for an indefinite run. But, he explained, riverboat entertainment was all the rage now, and the cast played to standing-room audiences every weekend.

Jessie rejoined Ki and told him that after they had met with Dr. Whitaker, she had plans to drop by her actress friend's rooms for a long-overdue get-together. She was certain Ki could take care of matters without her. Ki agreed

45

to take the surgeon back to his home and retrace the path to each of the murder sites.

When Dr. Whitaker and his police shadow arrived together at the hotel, there was a replacement waiting for them. Captain Bernard, hoping to see Jessica, had assigned himself as Detective Jeggi's relief. He stood on the curb, off to the side, watching as the doorman helped Dr. Whitaker down from his carriage. To the chief of detectives' utter astonishment, Detective Jeggi alighted from the same carriage, almost directly on the heels of the surgeon.

Captain Bernard yanked the exhausted plainclothesman off to one side and demanded, "What in hell do you think you're doing, Johnnny, riding *with* the doctor! You're supposed to be following him—keeping him under surveillance—not accompanying him!"

The bedraggled police detective whined, "Somehow they found me out and invited me to join them last night. I could not very well pretend I was not following him, and I thought it better to stay with him than to lose him."

Through clenched teeth Captain Bernard said, "Detective Jeggi, your eighteen hours are up. I'll take over from here. You did watch him all night, did you not?"

Unwilling to admit his transgression, the plainclothesman said, "Oh, yes, sir. I kept a close eye on him. Stayed with him like glue—never out of my sight. Except, of course, when he went to bed. But I had a clear view of the main staircase the whole time."

"Good. Now go home and get some sleep—you look terrible!" Captain Bernard said, following the surgeon into the hotel lobby.

Jessica recognized Captain Bernard even before she saw Dr. Whitaker, and she could not help but notice how pleased she felt to see him. And from the look on the chief of detectives' face as he surveyed her lavender taffeta and lace

46

gown with matching bonnet and handbag, he was equally happy to see her.

"Good morning, Captain," Jessie said warmly. "And a good morning to you, Doctor. Did you have a good sleep in your own bed for a change?"

"Thank you, yes," Dr. Whitaker said as he avoided making eye contact with Captain Bernard. His emotions were still smarting from the impersonal inquisition suffered at the hands of the chief of detectives while in jail. "Good morning, Ki," he said, pointedly ignoring the police captain and extending his hand to Ki.

Ki responded, "Good morning, both of you." He looked around. "Where is Detective Jeggi? Have we lost him?"

"I have relieved him," said the police captain. "It is my turn to tail Dr. Whitaker." He smiled and brazenly appraised Jessica's beauty. "You look even lovelier this morning than yesterday," he said, reaching for her lace-gloved hand and brushing it lightly with his lips.

Jessie tried to ignore the shock of sexual desire that accompanied that brief kiss. "Thank you, kind sir," she said half in jest. She found it difficult to take her eyes off his. In fact, it was becoming increasingly difficult to concentrate. Forcing herself to clear her mind of sensual thoughts, she said, "If it's all right with you, Captain, Ki is going to take Dr. Whitaker back to his house to retrace his path to both murder victims' rooms."

The police captain replied, "That is a sound plan, but if Ki is going to be with Dr. Whitaker, my presence would be all but superfluous." His gaze penetrated Jessie to her soul as he said, "I am certain my time could be better spent going over the case with you, Miss Starbuck. Your reputation precedes you."

To Ki, Jessie said, "I'll be at Joy Madison's from ten o'clock on, should you need me for anything. You have her address, don't you?"

Ki smiled and nodded. "Yes. Enjoy your visit."

To Dr. Whitaker she said, "You are in the best possible hands. If there's anything at all to be learned, Ki will find it. And should anyone attempt to harm you, his ability to protect you is unmatched. Please don't be misled by his apparent lack of weapons." She smiled and winked a farewell to Ki.

Finally, as Ki and the surgeon turned to depart, Jessica said to the chief of detectives, "Police headquarters is so far away." She smiled and tilted her head. "There's an extremely comfortable suite of rooms at our disposal right here, Captain."

"Curt—please call me Curt."

"And you may call me Jessica," she whispered enticingly.

Her green eyes gleamed as Curt followed her up the grand staircase at a discreet distance. She could see both their reflections in the massive floor-to-ceiling mirrored wall at the head of the first landing. She turned and slowly climbed the elegantly carpeted stairs to the right of the landing, looking down over the balustrade at the police detective.

As Curt reached the landing, he turned to the left, ascending the other parallel staircase. They would meet on the second floor.

In the second-floor corridor, away from onlookers who might construe this for exactly what it was, Jessica waited and held out a delicately gloved hand to Curt as he climbed the last step and approached her. His long fingers enveloped her tiny hand and held it firmly, yet tenderly.

Jessie caught her breath as the exciting electricity of his touch—even on her gloved hand—surged through her again. Their eyes never strayed, locked intently on the other's. Finally they would both satisfy the inner curiosity that had nagged at them from the moment they met. An urge greater than either of them drew them to the suite and past the foyer.

Alone in the large central drawing room, the couple circled each other, enjoying the pleasure of their senses. Jessica took off her bonnet and gloves, and Curt took both her hands in his and kissed the soft, fleshy palms. Then he sucked one of her delicate fingertips into his warm mouth. Tingles of passion shot through her, and she squirmed with delight.

She looked deep into his eyes, noticing the tiny flecks of white and deep blue that swam in the crystal-blue. The whites of his eyes crisply contrasted, creating a startling effect. Long, dark blond lashes fringed his lids, as beautiful as any woman's, Jessica thought, yet quite fitting on this extremely masculine man.

As she placed her arms around his neck, Curt pulled the bone pins from her long honey-blond curls until strands of silken hair hung about her shoulders and down her back. He wound his hand into her hair and pulled her face close to his. His moist lips brushed hers ever so lightly, then pressed harder, his tongue delicately tracing the outline of her luscious lips.

Jessie responded immediately. She sighed as her tongue reached out to meet his, her arms clinging tightly to him. His musky scent intoxicated her, and she breathed in deeply, drinking in his maleness. She could feel his desire thrusting at her through their layers of clothing. Without breaking the kiss, she reached back and unbuttoned her dress, then undid the buttons of his jacket. As her gown slid off her shoulders, Curt kissed her neck gently, then licked her delicious flesh down to her shoulder, his tongue flicking her throat seductively.

Her fingers fumbled as she pulled at her petticoats and camisole. She stepped out of her many folds of lace and cotton and stood in her proud nakedness. Curt stood back a moment to admire the rosy fullness of her perfect breasts and dark pink nipples, the remarkable curve of her tiny waistline, and the inviting swell of her voluptuous hips. The dainty triangle of blond fur between her legs seemed to beckon to him. He tore at his trousers, pulling the buttons open, kicking off his boots.

They both stood for a moment, staring appreciatively at the other's inviting body, taunting their desire by remaining apart. Jessica marveled at the symmetry of Curt's muscular frame, the masses of curly light-brown chest hair encircling his tiny pale nipples. At least six feet tall barefooted, he towered over her without overpowering her. His sensuous erection bobbed slightly, its massiveness weighing it down.

Jessica caressed him with her body, stroking his thigh with hers. Then she took his swollen member seductively in her hand and moved her fingers up and down the shaft. Curt moaned as his knees nearly buckled, and he cupped her breasts in his palms. Jessie wrapped a hand around his neck and pulled his head down, thrusting a nipple into his mouth. As his tongue and lips covered her delicious flesh, she groaned and swayed.

Curt could endure no more, so he scooped her up into his arms and carried her to the nearest chesterfield. In one motion he placed her on the cushions and was on top of her, his hot flesh pressing down on hers. Her legs encircled his body as she took hold of the sensitive head of his manhood and guided it to her moistness. Dipping her thumb in her passion fluids, she massaged the tip of his erection until he yelped with pleasure. Then she slipped him inside her, just a little at first to tantalize him all the more.

He nipped playfully at her firm breasts, biting her nipples and teasing them with his tongue. Her hips swayed and her inner muscles caressed him. Deeper and deeper he plunged, until he was in up to the hilt. He pulled himself out slowly, deliciously, then thrust himself in fully again. As their passion built, they rolled from side to side, finally tumbling off the chesterfield and onto the thick carpet. Their desire built furiously as they rolled over, with Jessie on top, then Curt.

With a soft cry of ecstasy, Jessie's body throbbed and pulsed as Curt's shaft plunged into her again and again, finally filling her with hot fluids. They laid there, still entwined, tightly embraced yet completely relaxed. Curt looked down and kissed the tip of Jessie's pert nose.

"God, you're beautiful!" he said, sighing contentedly as he felt himself begin to stir again between her legs.

Chief Carstairs had been widowed for almost a year. His Jenny had given him two strapping sons and a lovely, fragile daughter and had made his life a lot more tolerable than most. She had absorbed all his worries, all his tensions, and she had hidden her physical ailments from him. Jenny had never been one to complain or draw attention to herself. She had lived for her husband and her children, and when the boys went off to fight in the War between the States, she had nearly died of heartache and worry.

She had also almost died of sorrow when their daughter married a wanderer who wanted to blaze new trails. Her greatest pain was that she never knew if they were grandparents, because neither son returned from the war, and they lost touch with their daughter and her husband after the couple reached Denver. The Carstairs were never notified of a death, but as the years passed and no word came, hope grew faint and finally flickered and died. The pain of presumed loss had been almost more than Jenny could bear, but she had never let her husband see her grieve. She devoted her life to his happiness, making him feel special and loved.

When Jenny died, the police chief buried himself in his work and his hounds. Living way out in the country on a large parcel of land surrounded by a sassafras orchard, he spent what little free time he had hunting with his hounds. Jasper, Felix, and Archie were all he had left. They were his babies now, his children, a way of giving and receiving affection. They greeted him wildly when he finally dragged himself home each night after fourteen or sixteen long hours at headquarters. They made it all worthwhile.

The mayor and several of the chief's closest friends in the department had been trying to convince him to give up the place in the country and move closer to his work, but the police chief insisted that his hounds were not city dogs. Just knowing they were there waiting for him to come home each night made his frustrating job bearable.

That evening, when Hiram Carstairs reined in the horse in front of his house and stepped from his carriage, the hair on the back of his neck stood on end. He did not have to be told something was amiss—he felt it deep in his gut. The hounds were silent. There was no greeting, no frenzy of welcome. The chief slowly drew his revolver and cocked it, ready for trouble.

Carefully placing one foot in front of the other, he tiptoed around the side of the house. It was too dark to see, and there were no lights on in the house—which was as it should be. He lived alone, and the only lights that shone would be the ones he himself lighted.

He stopped and listened. An owl hooted, wings fluttered, and something small rustled in the brush by the old oak tree. It was too cold for frogs and crickets, but a few night birds sounded out in the orchard. Somewhere way off in the distance, a hound bayed, but it wasn't Jasper or Felix or Archie—the chief knew their howls, each so individual, so distinctive, so familiar.

As he rounded the corner of the house and entered the backyard area, he sniffed the air, smelling something familiar—gunpowder. Cautiously, he made his way toward the back porch, feeling each footstep on the flagstone walkway. As he reached the house, he stumbled over something firm yet giving. Righting himself before he fell, he backed off a step and struck a match.

In the soft glow he saw the sprawled bodies of Jasper and Felix, their heads blown to smithereens. The chief dropped to his knees, a cry of anguish slicing through the peaceful countryside. Startled night birds fluttered and flew away, and tiny critters scurried for cover as the almost inhuman wail continued.

Finally gathering his composure, Hiram Carstairs opened the back porch door and reached inside for a lantern. Lighting it, he surveyed the area. There was no one there, but whoever had shot his hounds had just left. The lingering scent of gunpowder told him so.

Why had the killer left without ambushing him? Why had someone so brutally killed Jasper and Felix? And where was Archie?

Chief Carstairs held the lantern low so he could check the area for evidence. Suddenly he was on duty again, surveying the scene of a dastardly crime. Where was Archie? Next to the blood splattered around Jasper and Felix was a large pool of darkened congealing liquid that trailed off into the darkness. From the position of the two hounds' bodies, the trail of blood could not have been theirs. They had obviously died instantly. Archie must have been wounded and hauled himself off to die.

"Archie!" Chief Carstairs called out. "Hey, boy, where are you, feller?" He whistled and patted his pantleg and clicked his tongue. "Come on, boy, where you hidin'? Don't worry, it's me."

A small critter rustled the bushes nearby and another owl hooted—or was it the same one? Then Chief Carstairs's heart jumped as he heard a low wheeze and a soft, almost inaudible whimper coming from the direction of the old root cellar. He held the lantern high as he rushed through the shadows toward the mound of earth.

There, huddled in the overgrown entrance to the disused root cellar, big eyes glowing red in the lanternlight, was Archie. Blood crusted to the neck and shoulder, the wounded hound lay quietly, the tip of its tail making an attempt to wag, big brown eyes searching his master's face for a reason for so much pain.

Chief Carstairs resisted the urge to grab the hound up in his arms and hug him for joy. The pain would probably kill the dog. Instead, he rushed to the pump and primed it, hauling up a steady stream of cool water. Soaking his handkerchief first, he then caught water in his hat, bringing it to the badly mangled hound.

Gently, lovingly, he bathed away the encrusted blood and examined the wounds more carefully. From what he could tell, the shots had hit no vital organs. He carefully scooped the dog up and carried him into the house, placing him on his big double bed. He would get Doc Bartlett in the morning, but he would not leave Archie's side that night—not even to fetch the vet.

Chief Carstairs choked back a sob of rage as he gingerly hauled the dead hounds' carcasses into the enclosed back porch area to protect them from scavengers. Then he turned his attention to Archie as he tended to the wounds.

With care and time, he hoped in a silent prayer, Archie would be almost as good as new. And once Archie was fully healed, the dog would be ready to hunt again. But this time the hound would be hunting down the killer who had murdered Jasper and Felix.

Chapter 6

Bertha Schultz stopped in her tracks. The smell was horrific—something had obviously died. She was a little late this morning—she usually arrived much earlier to make Chief Carstairs's breakfast and tidy up the house after he had left for headquarters.

But today she had had to tend to two of her own children before leaving the house. Both were down with croup, and she had worked for the Carstairs long enough to know the chief would not mind her tardiness. Especially since his wife had passed on, the chief had been very grateful for whatever she did—and most generous, too.

The stench of death grew stronger as she approached the back of the house. She hurried to get inside, away from the putrid foulness hanging heavy in the morning air. She held her breath as she pushed open the back door to the porch. She stopped short. What was left of Jasper and Felix blocked her path. She dropped her purse and bag and threw up her arms. Her scream could be heard two houses away as she shrieked in horror.

Chief Carstairs, who had been too preoccupied with Archie to remember to cover the dead hounds or move them away from the door, suddenly recalled the cleaning lady as her screams pierced his bedroom and awakened him. He had been up most of the night with Archie and had only just nodded off when the woman began her terrified bawling.

Now he realized as he shook himself awake that the poor woman probably thought he, too, had been murdered. Checking first to assure himself that Archie was breathing normally and sleeping easily, Chief Carstairs lumbered down the stairs as quickly as he could, calling out to the frightened woman as he came.

"Mrs. Schultz, I'm all right. Please, Mrs. Schultz—Bertha—I'm here."

He opened the inner door to the back porch and called to her again, but she was in such a state of shock that his presence did not penetrate her awareness. She kept right on shrieking, pulling at her hair, stomping her feet, and screeching in German between screams.

"Mrs. Schultz—Bertha!" he yelled with all the authority he could muster. "Stop it! I am here. I'm perfectly all right."

Finally his words got through to her, and she ceased her screaming. She whimpered quietly, backing away from the two dead hounds.

Chief Carstairs held out his arms, and the stocky woman edged her way around the bodies and rushed to him, encircling his waist with her beefy arms. She sobbed softly on his chest until she had calmed down enough to catch her breath. Then she grabbed him by the face and kissed both his cheeks.

"Oh, thank the God you are not killed!" she said in a thick German accent. "I think for certain you are dead, too. Oh, thank the God you are alive!" Her red swollen eyes looked up at him as she waited for an explanation.

"Last night before I got home," he said haltingly, "someone shot Jasper and Felix to death and badly wounded Archie. Whoever did it was not here when I arrived. But I didn't miss the bastard by much. There was still gunpowder in the air." He spoke more to himself than to the cleaning lady. Then he remembered her and said, "Mrs. Schultz, I hate to ask, but would you please go for Doc Bartlett? Archie needs a vet, and I don't want to leave him here until I am sure he is all right.''

''*Ach, ja!*'' she replied, falling into her native tongue as she turned and ran down the flagstone path. ''*Bitte*, uh, please, I be right back with Herr Doctor Bartlett. Oh, *Mein Gott*, who would do this?''

Captain Curt Bernard left the hotel and waited outside on the street. Minutes later Jessica joined him on the sidewalk. The chief of detectives had insisted on preceding her to preserve her reputation, and she had agreed only to humor him. She had donned a pale turquoise wool suit, more appropriate for a visit to her friend Joy on such a chilly late-autumn morning.

''May I call you a cab, sir?'' the doorman asked stiffly.

Captain Bernard said quickly, ''Please.'' He turned to Jessica. ''May I at least drop you off at your friend's place? I'm sure it isn't that much out of my way.''

Jessie took a slip of paper from her hangbag and showed it to him. ''It's near Eads Bridge—'' She broke off, laughing. ''But I don't have to tell you that. You must know all of St. Louis like the palm of your hand.''

He nodded and helped her into the carriage the doorman had summoned. ''Your friend's address is just a few blocks from here.'' He called out the cross streets to the cabbie and settled back, Jessica's hand cradled in his.

As Jessie looked out at the passing scenery, Curt pointed out the sights, indicating the courthouse, the public library, and the construction site for the city's newest and tallest building.

''We call it a skyscraper,'' he said proudly. ''It's going to be ten stories high.''

''Ten stories?'' Jessie marveled, examining the partially completed steel structure as they passed.

The carriage came to a stop in front of a modest row of brick houses, some painted, some left natural. The police captain called out the exact street number to the cabbie, but refused to release Jessie's hand. She smiled and leaned toward him, kissing him softly on the cheek. He took her in his arms and kissed her soundly before jumping down and assisting her from the carriage.

"I would insist on staying with you," he said sincerely, "but I wouldn't presume to intrude on your reunion—and I have work to do and a slasher to catch." His smile looked troubled. "And a burglar or two and a few ruffians, as well as a couple of vigilante groups to contend with."

Jessica turned to go. "I'm sure I will see you later."

"Dinner?" he said, not really asking. "I'll pick you up at your hotel at seven-thirty."

His smile nearly blinded her. How could she refuse him anything? "Fine. I'll see you then."

Jessica turned again and headed into the front yard of the address her friend had given. It was a two-story brick house painted gray. The directions said to walk around to the rear and up the stone staircase there. She followed the gravel pathway to the back of the dwelling and stopped at the foot of a steep set of stone steps leading to a second-floor door.

As she mounted the steps, she wondered if she would recognize Joy. The actress had become quite famous, and it had been a long time since they had seen each other. Would Joy recognize her? She would find out in just a moment. Excited anticipation caused her to bounce up the last few steps and rap eagerly on the private door. Jessie's gloved knuckles made almost no sound, so she removed her glove and banged away with bare fist.

No response.

Jessica knocked again, a little harder this time. Joy had never been one to oversleep before, she thought, glancing at her silver-and-turquoise lapel watch. Had she been called away, she would most certainly have left a note on the door or sent a message to the hotel. Jessie banged louder, calling out her friend's name.

Still no response.

She took a double-eagle coin from her handbag and rapped with the edge of it as loudly as she could. "Joy! Are you there? It's Jessie!"

A downstairs window flew open, and a head full of rag curlers popped out. "Fer crissake, are you tryin' to raise the dead! What's all the racket up there?"

Jessie leaned over the side of the stairs. "I'm very sorry if I've disturbed you, but I have an appointment with Miss Madison, and she doesn't appear to be answering." She smiled at the pudgy woman. "Did you by any chance see her leave?"

"No, I did not. Do I look like a busybody?" Her voice held an edge of defensiveness. "And she didn't come down to breakfast this morning, either."

"But Miss Madison asked me to meet her here at ten. It's after that now, and she doesn't seem to be home. Quite frankly, I'm more than a little concerned."

The middle-aged woman shook her head, then changed her mind and said, "All right. Don't get in a snit. I'm sure ever'thing's hunky-dory. But if you're all that insistent, come on down and we'll try from inside."

Jessica went to the door once again and tried to peer in the window off to one side. She could just make out a bed and a lamp on a side table. But from where she stood, it was impossible to see if anyone was there. She turned and retraced her steps to the front of the house. The large woman who had called to her stood in the doorway in a well-worn housecoat.

"This way," she said, as if rendering the world's greatest favor.

"I do appreciate this, and I apologize for any inconvenience, but I am rather worried." Jessica followed the older woman up a narrow flight of stairs and down a long dark hallway that smelled of age. "By the way, my name is Jessica Starbuck."

"Yes? How nice, I'm sure." Without even looking back, the hefty woman said, "And I'm Mrs. O'Callaghan, the owner of this here boardinghouse."

At the last door on the right the woman stopped and banged hard on number 25. When there was no answer, she kicked the door with her foot several times. The door of number 24 across the hall came open a crack, as did number 23 next door. Two heads peered out and watched silently.

"All right, now," Mrs. O'Callaghan said sarcastically, "there ain't no show going on here. You can both go back to whatever you was doin'."

"No, wait! Please!" Jessie cried. "Did either of you see Miss Madison this morning?"

Both doors closed almost in unison. Bolts clicked into place.

Mrs. O'Callaghan smirked. "Well, I'll tell Miss Madison you was here when she gets in." She turned and started back down the hall.

Jessica refused to budge. "Something is very wrong here. Joy would have sent me a message or left a note, but she didn't. Please, Mrs. O'Callaghan. She may be ill or hurt. Could you open the door?"

The large woman shook her head as she approached the top of the stairs, her back to Jessie.

Still at number 25, Jessie called down the corridor, "She might have tripped, fallen, and hit her head. She might have fainted, perhaps she needs medical attention. You must have a key."

The woman hesitated and looked back, studying Jessica from the head of the stairs.

Almost pleading, Jessie said, "What would be the harm

in looking? If she's not in, she'll never know; if she's inside and in need of help, she'll thank you. She would be extremely grateful—and so would I.'' She opened her handbag and rummaged in it.

Mrs. O'Callaghan dug into her housecoat pocket and withdrew a number of keys on a string. Sweating from exertion, the large woman stopped in front of Jessie and asked, "How grateful?"

Jessie took out a coin and handed it to the woman and watched as the key turned in the lock.

Mrs. O'Callaghan tried to fling open the door, calling out Joy's name as she did, just in case. But something was propped against the door, making it almost impossible to open. The boardinghouse owner put her chunky shoulder to the door and shoved hard. The door gave a little, opening just a crack. Something was definitely blocking the doorway. With a loud grunt, the hefty woman gave it all she had, and the door swung open as something heavy thumped inside the room.

Peering around the corner of the door, Mrs. O'Callaghan looked in. Then she gasped and shrieked bloody murder as she clutched her mouth and heaved into her hands. She stumbled backward, blocking Jessie's view of the room, and fell in a dead faint at the honey-blonde's feet.

Jessie started to go to Mrs. O'Callaghan's aid, but now the room was visible. There on the floor, lying in a pool of dried blood, was a garishly made-up dead body of a young woman. A blond wig with masses of long curls had been pulled askew, displaying neutral brown hair underneath. The painted lips seemed frozen in a silent scream. Long black fake lashes framed open, staring eyes. The scene was grotesque beyond anything Jessie could have imagined.

Her stomach turned as she sagged against the doorway for support. Someone had slit this poor woman's throat. And she had either been trying to get out through the hallway door or the murderer had propped her up against the door. But who was she? She was obviously a lady of the evening. Where was Joy? Was this Joy? With all the blood and heavy makeup, and the death grimace, it would be difficult to recognize anyone. Jessica did not want it to be her friend lying dead, but the body was the right size, and the bone structure resembled Joy's.

She was barely aware of the crowd in the hallway as she stood gazing at the blood-spattered room. Blood was everywhere—the bed was dappled with dark red spots, the floor, the side table. Even the lamp Jessie had seen from the outside held splashes of dried blood.

Suddenly Jessie felt ridiculous, almost helpless, in her city garb. Somehow this murder scene called for action. She wanted to be in her jeans—with her Colt strapped to her hip. She had to do something, anything. Even if that was not Joy lying there, it was someone—someone who had been brutally murdered. She stood in the doorway, gaping, taking in the entire room, her mind automatically sorting and filing every grisly detail, every possible clue.

Under her breath she mumbled, "That *can't* be Joy. It just can't!" It didn't make sense. Nothing did. She turned from the room, took a deep breath, and saw a gathering crowd of roomers clustered in a semicircle around the door, some staring at the fainted landlady, most trying to get a good look at the body beyond the door. Jessica motioned the curiosity-seekers, back, looking from face to face, and said, "Don't just stand there! Send for the police! Somebody get the police!"

Sergeant Hobbs took the stairs two at a time. Why him? Why his neighborhood? This was the third slashing in almost as many weeks, and his stomach still was not accustomed to it. But when he got to the room, he saw that this one was a little easier to take. At least the poor dear was still fully dressed. That was different from the other two. He was certain the captain would make something of that. He blocked off the corridor and asked everyone to go downstairs until the chief of detectives could question them.

The one called Jessica Starbuck was the only person there who did not seem to belong. Her fine clothing and genteel bearing told him more than she could in words. Although she wanted to stay, to assist, Sergeant Hobbs insisted she go down to the drawing room with the others and wait until the captain arrived.

Mrs. O'Callaghan finally came around and found enough strength to make it down the stairs under her own steam with the help of Jessie's strong shoulder. Badly shaken, the sweaty older woman plopped herself on the overstuffed chesterfield and sat fanning herself with a dirty hankie. Jessica found a tattered loveseat and perched on the edge of it—waiting.

No more than ten minutes after Sergeant Hobbs arrived, Captain Bernard strode through the front door. He walked past the crowd into the drawing room and looked around the room, his crystal-blue eyes searching for Jessica. Seeing her, he rushed to her side.

"What happened?" Noting her ashen cheeks, he asked, "It wasn't your friend, was it?"

"I don't know. It appears to be some, uh, lady of the evening, but I couldn't be sure. I guess I just don't want it to be her. But if it isn't Joy, and I pray it isn't, then where is she? Whatever the case maybe, there's a dead woman in Joy's room, horribly slashed."

Captain Bernard sent Hobbs for Chief Carstairs and then went up to examine the murder scene. He had gone over everything thoroughly by the time the chief arrived.

"Well, Curt, what do we have here?" the chief demanded as he barged through the doorway of number 25 and looked around the grisly scene.

Lowering his voice so as not to be overheard, the police captain said solemnly, "Another slasher victim. But also a case of mistaken identity."

"Now, what do you mean by that?"

"Well, Chief, at first glance, it looks as if we got ourselves another whore. But this one is fully dressed, including her cloak and hat and gloves. And her string handbag is still around her wrist." He held up a handful of papers. "I pieced together her identity from these. They were in her purse—a letter and a note from a friend, some tickets to a play."

The chief riffled through them.

Captain Bernard continued, "As you can see, the dead woman *is* Joy Madison. She was starring in that melodrama at the Floating Palace—and she was a close friend of Jessica Starbuck's."

The chief studied the murdered woman's face. "Well, if she wasn't a whore, then what the hell was she doing made up like one?"

"The way I see it, I bet she didn't bother to take off her makeup at the theater last night. The steamboat is moored just a few blocks from here near Ead's Bridge."

The chief nodded, remembering pleasanter times spent on the big paddlewheeler.

Continuing, the police captain said, "That would explain why this one was still clothed while the other two were not. The slasher thought he had another easy woman and was planning to have a night of it before carving her up. But this time he made a mistake. I could be wrong, sir, but I think our local ripper is imitating London's madman."

The chief smiled wryly, scratching his chin with the mouthpiece of his pipe. "You might be right—unless it *is* London's ripper!"

Chapter 7

The public's outcry at the third slashing greatly intensified when it was discovered that the police had had an extremely likely suspect in their grasp and had set him free—on $100,000 bond—just hours before the murder.

From their front pages, both the St. Louis *Post-Dispatch* and the *Globe-Democrat* cried for the resignation of Chief Carstairs and demanded the recall of Mayor Palmer. Smaller weeklies went much further; some actually suggested a hanging or two would solve everything. Editorials pointed out that not even guests in their fair city were safe. The brutal slaying of someone as famous as actress Joy Madison enflamed the citizens of St. Louis, uniting them with a common purpose—the detection and destruction of the Mad Ripper.

The *Post-Dispatch* offered a $2,000 reward for information leading to the capture and conviction of the Ripper; their competition matched the reward; and Mayor Palmer and the city council offered another $1,000. With $5,000 at stake, passions heightened and vigilante groups moved freely through the city policing the public, stopping anyone who looked the least bit suspicious to them.

Several hefty brewery workers, reading in the weeklies that the police suspected anyone who earned a living with a sharp instrument, decided to make their own investigation. They went from block to block, demanding alibis and witnesses from every surgeon, veterinarian, butcher, and barber they came upon.

Jenda Leng, a German immigrant who had been a local butcher for nearly twenty-two years, balked at the mobs' questions. He felt his reputation in the neighborhood held him in good stead, and he knew these men had no authority to interrogate or bully him.

"You have no right to question me! I tell you nothing! I told the police, but you I tell nothing!" the middle-aged butcher shouted in contempt.

"That's what you think, Fritz!" yelled one of the largest of the group. His fist slammed into Leng's stomach, doubling the slight man over in pain.

Another bruiser growled, "You better tell us where you were, Heinzie! Tell us—or else!" His fist caught the butcher on the chin, knocking the man reeling and his wire-rim spectacles flying.

Onlookers gasped and women screamed, but the gang held firm, demanding an alibi. Their self-righteousness was their badge of authority as they pushed and shoved Leng from one brute to another.

"I tell you nothing! You are scum, swine!" Leng whispered, sucking blood from his lip.

As Leng's wife and neighbors watched, the burly vigilantes hauled the bloodied man off down the street. "We know what to do with murderers!" one beefy lout yelled.

"I kill no one! You are all crazy! Let me go!" His feet barely touched the ground as the huge men on either side of him dragged him along. He smelled the liquor on them— they had been drinking, and he knew there was no reasoning with them. "Help! Police!"

The bully on the right hit him hard in the side of the face. "Shut up! You don't wanna tell us nothing? Well, Fritz, we're gonna teach you some manners. When we're finished, you ain't gonna tell nobody nothing." He grinned and looked at the others. "Right, boys?"

Leng's tongue massaged his loosened teeth, and he swallowed blood. His mind raced ahead, trying to think of some way of escaping this mob of hoodlums. Pain surged through his head—until he saw the rope. Suddenly he felt nothing but pure terror.

The biggest bruiser of the group held a noose high overhead and waved it about. The rest cheered. They looked around for something to toss it over.

"That lamppost over there should do just fine!" he yelled.

"No! My God, no!" Jenda Leng cried, his knees giving way under him. "I'll tell you whatever you want—anything, please!"

As the big man slipped the noose around the butcher's neck, he laughed. "Too late, Fritz!" He tossed the other end high over the sturdy metal protrusion.

The mob, satisfied, left the bloodied butcher dangling from the lamppost, his sightless eyes bulging and his tongue purple and swollen.

Other gangs roamed the streets looking for suspects, tossing bricks and rocks through windows of butcher and barbershops and ransacking physicians' surgeries. There were not enough police to go around, and panic set in.

Clark Buttrick coveted the reward money for many reasons, most important of which was his desire for position and power. A medical school dropout with more aptitude for drink than for medicine, he still harbored his dream of being a famous physician. Long gone, though, were any thoughts of helping and healing. His only motive was to attain the rewards incumbent with fame and power—a mansion in Vandeventer Place and a social status denied him by birth.

Buttrick and his mob carried torches as they marched down the center of Market Street. They had already served notice on the police that they were going to handle the Mad Ripper themselves. They were certain they knew who the mass murderer was—Dr. Louis Whitaker—but they were unable to gain entrance to the gated Vandeventer Place section. Had they been able to break through the guarded entrance, they would have laid ruin to the surgeon's mansion. The mob was not aware of their leader's blind desire to raze what he could not possess.

Frustrated by their futile attempt to overrun the surgeon's home, they headed for his surgery downtown. They found it deserted and demolished it, confiscating all surgical instruments.

Then, with Buttrick leading, the rabble stormed the doors of police headquarters, barging on through to the front desk. Sergeant Laymon and two of his men confronted the mob.

"You looking to get yourself arrested, Buttrick!" The sergeant stood with feet spread apart and hands on hips, his right not far from his holster.

"We come for that murderer Whitaker," Buttrick bellowed and tried to move past the sergeant. "He's gotta be here. He ain't at home, and he ain't at his surgery. Give him to us, or we'll get him ourselves!"

Someone in the crowd waved a noose overhead, and several men drew their weapons. The blazing torches, raised high, scorched the dirty ceiling and threatened to set fire to the building.

Sergeant Laymon stood his ground as his men drew their weapons and cocked them. Buttrick glared at the impediment. This sergeant was making a fool of him.

"Give us Whitaker!" he yelled. "Dammit, Laymon, give us Whitaker!"

The mob echoed their leader. "Give us Whitaker!" someone shouted from the back.

Suddenly it became a chant. The entire mob as one man

68

called, "Give us Whitaker! Give us Whitaker! Give us—"

A shot cracked the air, silencing the mob. Captain Bernard held a revolver high above his head and shouted, "Dammit! Get the hell out of here, Buttrick! And take your friends with you!"

Buttrick had had only a few beers, so he could still reason. His inner rage could still be contained. But this man was humiliating him in front of his men. He could not let the affront go unchallenged; he had to do something quickly. There was too much at stake here, and the world was watching.

He sized up the situation—there were three uniformed policemen, the chief of detectives, an unarmed Chinaman, and a blond female. All he had to worry about were the ones with the guns, and only three of them had their weapons drawn. Sergeant Laymon was still just standing with his hands on his hips.

Buttrick grabbed Laymon by an arm, spun him around, using the sergeant's body as a shield. With revolver in hand, he motioned to the captain. "Put your gun down or I shoot this one," he said as menacingly as he could. "I mean it!" He cocked his weapon and brought it to Laymon's ear, cramming it in. "All of you—drop 'em!"

"Buttrick, are you crazy?" Captain Bernard cried. "This is police headquarters, not some saloon. What are you trying to prove with this? Put down your gun and let the sergeant go—right now."

Buttrick laughed. "You got this all wrong, buster! I'm the one with a gun in this bastard's ear. You put down your gun and tell your boys to do the same, or my first bullet will be the last thing the sergeant hears!" His eyes told the chief of detectives he meant it.

Two men behind Buttrick cocked their weapons. Now Buttrick had the strength to back up his demand. Captain

Bernard surveyed the situation and realized that as things stood, he and his men were outnumbered unless he called for backup. The moment he did that, Laymon would be dead. And even if he could get off a shot at Buttrick or his men, two innocent bystanders would probably die in the crossfire. He could not jeopardize the welfare of Jessica and Ki.

"Buttrick," the chief of detectives said quietly, trying to reason, "we don't have Whitaker. He isn't here. All this is for nothing." He put his gun on the desk slowly, backing away from it, his hands in plain sight. "Come on, now. Let's talk about this calmly. We all want to find the slasher. But you're going about it all wrong."

He had no idea if Buttrick would react positively to his reasoning, but he had to chance it. He kept on speaking softly, urging the vigilante leader to let the hostage go.

Ignoring the captain's words, Buttrick looked from one uniformed policeman to the other and demanded, "All right, you two, drop 'em or I drop the sarge!" He raised his gun high and brought the barrel of it down sharply against Laymon's ear. Blood trickled down the sergeant's neck.

Both policeman looked to the captain. He nodded, and they placed their revolvers on the desk next to the captain's. The men behind Buttrick cheered, and the vigilante leader knew he had everything well under control. He was in command, and he was going to get the murdering bastard the police were protecting. He would get Whitaker from the police now—and string him up.

Swelled with power, Buttrick boldly shoved Laymon ahead of him as he edged forward, menacing all those standing in front of him. "Now, back off!" he ordered the two policemen.

The uniformed officers took several steps backward, obeying their captain's silent command.

Buttrick's head swam with power, and he felt he could

do anything. He motioned to Captain Bernard. "Come here, you bastard!"

As the chief of detectives opened his mouth to speak, he heard voices down the hall. Buttrick called to his men, assigning two of them to cover the door. The meanest of the mob moved to obey, guns drawn and cocked.

"I said, come here!" Buttrick said to the captain. "You want to see your sarge dead?"

Captain Bernard stepped forward, approaching Sergeant Laymon, a look of apology in his eyes directed at the hostage. He had sincerely hoped his reasoning would stop Buttrick, but he had only caused the situation to escalate. If he could somehow get the upper hand . . . but how?

Buttrick shoved the sergeant off to the side and grabbed Captain Bernard as his hostage. "Now, let's all jump to my tune, folks!" he crowed, a hearty laugh coming from his gut. "I want Whitaker, and I want him now!"

No one paid any attention to Ki and Jessica as, step by unnoticed step, they circled around either side of the scene and stood opposite each other almost parallel to Buttrick and his hostage. Jessica brought her hands up imperceptibly, held her handbag in front of her, and slowly slipped one hand inside.

Buttrick laughed harder, but the laughter caught in his throat as Ki's foot came up and snap-kicked the gun from the man's hand. The two bruisers covering the door brought their guns around, ready to fire.

Before either could squeeze the trigger, Jessie's Colt barked twice through the bottom of her handbag. Both men dropped their guns; blood dripping down their wrists as they yelped in pain.

Ki delivered a *nakadata* blow to the side of Buttrick's head just behind the ear. The man crumbled to his knees, then fell flat on his face, smashing his nose on the ungiving floor.

71

As Jessie held her Colt on the crowd, the two uniformed officers grabbed their weapons and tossed Captain Bernard his. But the added firepower was unnecessary. The vigilantes had changed from a powerful mob into a group of less interested men. Those nearest the front door turned tail and ran, dropping the torches and running for their lives, all thought of lynching gone.

Those not fast enough were herded off to spend time in the St. Louis jail. Buttrick was dragged to a solitary cell away from the others, and Sergeant Laymon went to have someone look at his ear.

Captain Bernard looked from Ki to Jessica and shook his head in disbelief. "Thank you, both of you. But was that an accident?" he asked Jessie, glancing down at her ruined handbag.

As Jessica's laughter tinkled through the room, Ki answered for her, "She was just a little off. I don't believe she meant to draw blood."

Chapter 8

The Reverend Arthur Bergendorfer, pastor of the First Lutheran Church of St. Louis in Vandeventer Place, looked out at the bedraggled drifters hunched on hard wooden benches at the Good Shepherd Rescue Mission at the corner of Washington and Fourth, and railed against the abominations of Demon Rum and John Barleycorn. The gaunt preacher ranted about the life of a wastrel and called upon the men to change their ways and come to the service of the Lord.

"If John Barleycorn doesn't get you, Demon Rum will—and you'll all fry in hell after your stomachs are rotted through!"

Father David Coolbaugh, founder of the mission and a defrocked priest, rolled his eyes ceilingward and wondered at how the pastor could reach middle-age with such a complete lack of understanding of his audience. These men sought shelter from the cold, a hot meal, and a bed of sorts for the night. Nothing more. They drifted from place to place, fending for themselves but accepting a handout once in a while. In return they sat and appeared to listen to sermons and threats and promises. They marked time until their next meal or snatches of sleep.

Warming to his theme, the upper-class minister broached his favorite topic—the sinner who had, within the past month, wantonly slain three young women. The preacher's thick German accent created harsh sounds as it sliced through his fluent English, echoing in the coldness of the small, barren river-district mission.

The tall clergyman chastised any in the audience who might think less of the slashing victims because of their professions, and he called on the entire group to rise up and do whatever they could to stop the killings. While he argued against vigilante action, he stressed that each of God's children had a purpose and, with a little effort, could somehow make a difference.

"Are we not all Christ's brethren?" he intoned piously. "And when one of Our Lord's lambs has gone astray, is it not the duty of His entire beloved flock to search out that errant lamb and bring it to justice—to slaughter if need be?"

Some of the men perked up at the word *slaughter*. But most of the drifters huddled on the hard seats and waited for the sermon to end. A few reasoned that the minister might be right. If the police could not hunt down the mad slasher—Reverend Bergendorfer's "stray lamb"—then someone must. For the protection of all women everywhere. Every woman in St. Louis appeared to be in jeopardy, and those living within the mission's territory near the docks seemed to be at extreme risk.

"From the front page of the *Globe-Democrat*, they would have us believe that one of our city's surgeons is most likely the vicious culprit!" the preacher exclaimed. "If this is indeed so, then we must find that surgeon and stop him before he slaughters every living female in St. Louis!"

A few of the men murmured assent.

Building to a crescendo of passion, the minister cried out, "But *is* the killer a local surgeon? What assurance do we have that this Mad Ripper, as the newspapers call him, is not in actuality London's Jack the Ripper?" He slammed his fist down on the podium so hard that those who dared doze jumped to full alertness. "*Post-Dispatch* editorials speculate that our city's slasher may indeed be Jack the Ripper! And why? Think! Did not the slashings in London, England, cease only a matter of weeks before our first poor lamb was slaughtered right here in St. Louis—in the United States of America?"

Some of the men sat alert, paying heed.

"Sweet little Daisy Dudler, one of your own dear neighbors, was the first victim—and she was a soiled dove. Consider! Were not all of Jack the Ripper's victims soiled doves?!"

Most of the drifters nodded, remembering what they had heard during Jack the Ripper's siege on London's tarts. Some of the more self-righteous in the audience smirked, and a few laughed out loud.

"They got what they deserved!" one old tosspot called out from the back.

"Judge ye not lest ye be judged!" the reverend boomed, shaking a long slender finger at the men. "Have you forgotten Mary Magdalene! Daisy Dudler may have chosen the world's oldest profession, but she was also a good friend to many of you as well as a faithful churchgoer. She did not deserve such an ugly death. Daisy will be sorely missed!"

His audience, many Daisy's customers, nodded solemnly.

"As some of you know, Daisy cared for everyone and loved the Lord. And although she may have been the only one of the three young murdered women who was a Lutheran, all three slashing victims lived within walking distance of this mission." He looked out accusingly at the saddened faces. "We must protect every woman in this dangerous neighborhood—it is our duty. If the police cannot find Daisy's murderer, we must!"

The men, usually silent during sermons, offered vocal agreement. "You are right!" "Yes!" "It is so!"

75

One lone voice up front asked, "But how?"

Pleased with the reaction, Reverend Bergendorfer laid his private theory before the group. "If all of us approach the people we know best, one at a time, we can cover the entire district inch by inch. No one need accept too large an area, as there are enough of us to spread throughout the vicinity and beyond." He smiled encouragingly. "It is so simple. Just warn all the women in the neighborhood personally, make them aware of the danger of going out alone at night They know already it is not safe, but offer to escort them — be a good neighbor, a good Christian—a good Lutheran— and save a life."

His audience appeared eager to make contact with the women in the wharf district. Usually interested in taking life one day at a time, they considered the benefits of coming to the aid of defenseless young women. The rewards could prove worth the effort.

Pounding again on the podium with all his might, Reverend Bergendorfer concluded, "We must find this mad slasher! I assure you, we can all make a difference—each one of us." His climax reached, he spoke softly. "And I myself will visit every soiled dove in the proximity of this mission." Again he smiled. "Perhaps I will save their souls and their lives at the same time."

At precisely nine o'clock the morning after Clark Buttrick's vigilante assault on police headquarters, Jessica Starbuck and Ki presented themselves, as requested, to the desk sergeant.

"We have an appointment with Chief Carstairs," Ki said, looking up at the large clock behind the policeman.

The sergeant nodded. "Yes, sir, ma'am. If you follow that corridor on the right, you'll find the chief's office— it's the last door on the left. Can't miss it." He could not

76

hide his admiration for the two and gave them a sharp salute as they passed by.

Jessica smiled appreciatively. "Thank you."

As the two made their way down the narrow hallway, the heels of Jessie's boots clacked loudly, while Ki's moccasins made no more than a faint whisper. Both had decided, after the vigilante confrontation of the night before, that they should wear their working attire whenever possible. They might be in the big city but it seemed a good idea to be prepared for the worst, since it was obvious that the situation in St. Louis was extremely grave, and the unexpected would now be commonplace.

As they approached the door on the left marked in gold lettering CHIEF OF POLICE, they heard a bellow from within.

"Hell and damnation! I said eat it!"

Jessie and Ki looked at each other for a moment before Ki knocked on the door and opened it, ushering Jessica in before him. Chief Carstairs looked up from his desk only momentarily. In his lap lay a large red-and-beige hound. The police chief was trying to get something down the dog's throat, obviously without much luck.

"Good morning, and thank you for coming," the police chief said warmly. "Please excuse me if I don't stand, but I'm trying to nurse Archie here back to health—and he's fighting me every inch of the way!" He stroked his hound lovingly as he spoke. "Come on in—sit." With his free hand he motioned to two sturdy wooden chairs.

"You wanted to see us, Chief?" Jessie asked, getting right to the point. She perched on the edge of her chair and waited expectantly, bracing herself for the barrage of condemnation she was sure would follow.

Ki lowered himself onto his chair and searched the chief's eyes for a clue to the reason for the summons.

"First of all, Miss Starbuck, I must apologize to you and your friend here. I did not realize who you were when I first met you. Please understand, these are not normal times here in St. Louis right now, and I had no idea you were *the* Jessica Starbuck of the Circle Star Ranch in Texas. Your exploits are almost as legendary as are your skills.'' He glanced in admiration at the Colt revolver holstered at her hip.

"Please call me Jessica. I'm sorry we were never formally introduced." She motioned toward Ki. "This is my associate, Ki.''

Ki nodded solemnly and waited.

"Well, Miss, uh, Jessica, now that we got the names straight, I'll get down to business." He scratched Archie behind the ears as he spoke. "I feel real bad about Joy Madison's death. Such a pretty gal and such a good actress. The world mourns her loss. It's a downright blasted shame that you lost such a close friend," he said in all sincerity, "—and spent a hundred thousand dollars doing it.''

That last bit of sarcasm was lost on neither Jessie nor Ki. It was a low blow, and Ki opened his mouth to say so. But the chief was not finished.

"Of course, from what I hear of the Lonestar empire, you can afford it.''

"Chief Car—" Ki began.

"Please . . .'' He waved Ki silent, directing his words to Jessica. "I'm not trying to be deliberately cruel. I'm sure you realize just how costly your grandstanding was. You not only endangered the entire city by arranging Dr. Whitaker's release, you also cost your friend her life. Of course, when you posted bail you had no idea Miss Madison would be his next victim. But she was, and you have only yourself and your fortune to blame.''

"If I may," Jessie said finally, "you are going on the assumption that Dr. Whitaker is guilty. We are equally as certain that he is not.''

Chief Carstairs shook his head. "Sure enough to bet your

and your stunt just might get your Dr. Whitaker hanged before he ever gets to trial!''

''All right, Chief,'' Jessie said contritely, holding back the enormity of her emotions, ''you've made your point. But I am sure you didn't summon us just to upbraid us.'' She swallowed hard. ''If Dr. Whitaker had remained in jail, his innocence would have been proved.'' Her voice turned brittle. ''And Joy would still be dead.''

The police chief knew they would never agree on this, so he pushed on. ''With three brutal killings, this city is near hysteria. You saw just a small portion of it last night.'' He looked from Jessie to Ki, his eyes pleading. ''We need help—I need help. These savage slashings are more than the St. Louis Police Department can handle. The entire situation is much too bizarre.''

The police chief reached over Archie for one of his pipes. As gingerly as he could, he balanced the ailing hound on his lap and tried to light the pipe. Finally Jessica struck a match and held it for him until his pipe was fully lighted.

Blowing thick blue smoke away from the dog, he puffed in silence for several long seconds. No one spoke. Jessie watched Archie's expressive pale liver-colored eyes, and Ki looked around the cluttered office, examining the many awards and commendations framed in black on the yellowed, peeling walls.

Finally Chief Carstairs cleared his throat and said, ''From what I've heard, you two are experts at handling the kind of problems we're having here in St. Louis.'' He hesitated, cleared his throat again, then rushed on. ''I guess, what I'm trying to say is—will you help us? I know you don't need the reward, but we sure as hell would be mighty appreciative!''

Jessie smiled, understanding just how difficult it must have been for the man to ask. ''Chief, even if I hadn't lost such a close friend, I would still have offered our expertise. Unless the slasher is caught soon, this situation can only escalate into something really ugly." She stood, adjusting her holster.

Ki got to his feet nodding.

"Ki and I are at your disposal," Jessie said, reaching over the desk to pat Archie's head. The dog whined gratefully and licked her hand. "We'll be more than happy, Chief, to work with you and Captain Bernard to rid your city of this madman."

"Good!" the police chief said, much relieved. "I was almost positive you would." He beamed at them both, then locked eyes with Jessica. "First thing—give us back Dr. Whitaker!"

Her gaze never wavered. "We don't have him. Your men are following him, so you should bring him in—for his own protection."

Ki added, "The public climate after the third murder has turned mean. Jessica is right—Dr. Whitaker would be much safer in jail, guilt or innocence aside."

Chief Carstairs pressed a button on the side of his desk. Less than a minute later Captain Bernard knocked and entered. "Yes, Chief?"

"These two say they don't have Dr. Whitaker. He's still under our surveillance, isn't he?" He continued without waiting, since his question was rhetorical. "Have your men bring—"

"Sir," the captain broke in, shaking his head, "we lost him." As he swallowed hard and readied himself for the chief's onslaught, he suddenly became aware of Jessica and Ki's anxious looks. He averted his eyes, looking straight ahead.

"You what!" The police chief yelled so loudly that his stomach bounced the hound in his lap. The startled dog jumped visibly and bayed.

The captain said, "Chief, Jeggi reported back this morning. Whitaker gave him the slip yesterday—right after the third slashing. We've looked everywhere for him—his house in Vandeventer Place, his surgery downtown, his club. We checked all his usual haunts and couldn't find him. He just seems to have disappeared. No one who knows him has seen him recently—or won't say."

The police chief flashed Jessica a "see what you've done" look and barked, "Find him, Curt! And that's an order!" As an afterthought, he added, "By the way, Miss Starbuck and Ki are going to be working with us on this." He smirked, turning to Jessica. "I don't know too many people who have a hundred thousand dollars to throw away, so I imagine you'll want to get out there and help find the doctor."

"Before Ki and I track the doctor down, perhaps you and the captain might let us know everything the police found at the murder scenes." She smiled, her voice purring, "That is, if we are to be of assistance."

Ki said, "I'm sure it won't take long."

The police chief nodded at Captain Bernard. "Curt, give 'em whatever they want." He looked down at Archie, stroked the hound's snout, and said, "Now, all of you, get out of here and let Archie have some rest."

Following the captain back to his office, Jessica and Ki said nothing. Jessica's concern for the surgeon's safety was apparent, and Ki tried to figure where someone as well-known as Louis Whitaker might find sanctuary.

After Captain Bernard showed Jessie and Ki all the paperwork on the slashings, Jessie asked, "Who visited Dr. Whitaker while he was in jail?"

"Hmmm, that's a good question." He riffled through a well-used notebook. "Warring, Waters, Weddington," he read off, thumbing through the pages. "Ah, here it is—Whitaker, Louis P., M.D. Just one visitor, on the day after he was brought in, then again every day thereafter—Priscilla Masters Whitaker, his ex-wife.'' He shook his head. ''But it says here that the doctor refused to see her after that first visit.''

Jessica said, ''Dr. Whitaker did say something to Ki and me about her trying to get him released on bail.'' She looked at the notebook. ''Does it show her address there?''

The captain read the scribbled entries carefully and finally said, ''Yes, here it is. Not a very good neighborhood.''

As the captain copied down the address for them, Jessica smiled at Ki, who nodded. They had their first destination on the trail of their client.

The cabbie stopped at the corner of Gratiot and Twenty-first, and Ki alighted ahead of Jessica, giving her a hand as she stepped down. As soon as she had both feet on the ground, the cabbie flicked the reins and made a quick exit, leaving the two standing in the street.

They surveyed the neighborhood and saw what Captain Bernard had meant. Disreputable-looking and rundown, both the buildings and the people, was the only way to describe it. A saloon on one corner, its swinging doors broken and hanging askew, told the tale. Several rough characters lounged in the doorway, and a brawl inside sounded as if it were about to burst out onto the street. The din of bottles shattering, furniture smashing, and savage punches meeting their mark spilled forth from the Red Fox Saloon.

With a loud crash, two burly toughs came flying out through the tavern doorway, fists pounding the other's body and face. Onlookers cheered as each blow slammed home. The smaller of the two reached from his knees and threw an uppercut that rocked the larger man to his heels. Blood spurted from the big man's nose, and he roared in pain and staggered toward his tormentor, fists flailing.

The smaller man, his arm cocked and ready to throw the punch that would end the argument, suddenly looked past his opponent and saw Jessica. In that split second the bigger man landed a crushing blow to the smaller man's groin with his boot, thrust his knee into the doubled-over man's face, and brought both fists down on the back of the man's neck, sending him sprawling. The downed man stayed down.

The rugged rooting section yelled their approval, hooting and whistling. Some called for the downed man to get back up and continue their entertainment. But he was out cold, face-down in the gutter.

One by one the men caught sight of Jessie and Ki—but no one looked at Ki. All eyes stared at the honey-blonde's tight jeans and form-fitting blouse. Her voluptuous breasts bounced sensuously as she walked, and the jeans hid none of the enticing sway of her rounded buttocks. The bruisers made appreciative noises and nudged one another, their primitive appetites whetted.

Jessie and Ki approached, walking down the sidewalk, apparently looking for a house number. Three of the ruffians took a step forward and filled the sidewalk, creating an impassable barrier of drunken muscle and flesh.

Suddenly aware of danger, Ki grabbed Jessie's arm and pulled her to a stop. He moved out in front of her slightly, stepping down off the curb with Jessica following. They tried to go around the toughs, which was what the bullies hoped they would do.

"Going somewhere, Chink?" the man with the big ears asked, glowering.

"Hey, there, perty gal," the man with his front teeth missing taunted, making kissing sounds.

The one with the big belly and no hair held out his hands to Jessica as if to squeeze her breasts. "Delicious—and ripe!" He smacked his lips obscenely.

Big Ears reached for Jessie's rounded buttocks, patting the air near her behind.

Ki turned to Jessie, bowing imperceptibly and winking. "Excuse me, ma'am," he said to her in mock gallantry, "but I have something to take care of. Please wait where you are. I won't be long."

In a flash Ki's foot slammed into the side of Big Ears' head, sending the thug into a heap in the gutter. Spinning around with lightning speed, Ki faced Toothless and delivered another *tobi-geri* kick to the ribs. The man reeled, and Ki slashed out with a chop to the neck. Toothless crumpled.

Before Big Belly could move, Ki spun again, his foot connecting with the fat man's chin with such force that the man sank to his knees, unconscious before his head hit the ground. Bystanders who might have joined in, stood back and whistled low.

Ki turned to Jessica, bowed again, and said, "Shall we proceed, m'lady."

Jessie giggled and stepped around the fallen toughs. "Thank you, good sir," she said with exaggerated dignity, trying to keep a straight face.

The two walked on down Graviot Street without any further disturbance, looking at house numbers until they found the one they wanted. Mounting the two wooden front steps, they both knocked on the door, looked at each other, and laughed.

From within, a woman's voice called out nervously, "Who is it?"

Jessica answered, "We're looking for Priscilla Masters Whitaker. My name is Jessica Starbuck."

The curtains at the front window parted, and someone peered out at Jessie and Ki, studying them carefully. Then the curtains fell back into place, and footsteps could be heard in the hallway. Bolts slipped out of their locks, a chain rattled, and the large brass doorknob turned.

With the door open a crack, a nose poked out as a pair of small, light-brown eyes with heavy lids surveyed the couple on the stoop. Finally assured of their identity, the plain woman stepped back and opened the door far enough for a person to pass through, saying, "Won't you please come in. I am Priscilla Whitaker."

Chapter 9

Thick knuckles rapped on the paint-peeled front door, at first tentatively, then insistently. Harriett Hartley opened one eye, listened for a moment, and waited. There it was again—some jackass was pounding on her door. If she lay still enough, maybe whoever it was would go away and she could get back to sleep.

Bam! Bam! Bam!

She jumped to her feet before she was fully awake, furious, her normally pallid ivory complexion blazing with color. How dare some sonuvabitch rouse her before sundown! None of her gentlemen would even think of disturbing her beauty sleep. She might not be quite twenty-two yet, but she still needed all the sleep she could get. She pushed aside her rich blue-black curls and looked at the clock on the chipped and gouged bureau—noon!—it was the middle of her night, for crissake!

Her Irish dander up, she grabbed a gawdy housecoat on the way to the door and jammed herself into it. She would definitely give whoever it was a royal piece of her mind! There was no excuse for waking her that way. Any regular customer of hers knew enough to wait till sundown.

Bam! Bam! Bam!

Harriett stopped dead in her tracks, bare feet chilled by the icy cold flooring. Her fists doubled and her peacock-blue eyes glared as her anger grew. She took a deep breath, trying to get control of herself, but the banging continued. The pounding was an obscenity, an invasion of her privacy that she should not be subjected to. The noise was just too much to take. She would flatten whoever it was!

Bounding forward without even asking who was there, she flung open the door, yelling, "You goddamn sonuv—" The words stuck in her throat as Harriett stood gaping, her jaw working with nothing coming out.

"Good day, Miss Hartley," said Reverend Bergendorfer, an apologetic half-smile frozen on his pale lips. He glanced at her robe. "I am very sorry—I take it you were napping"—he looked inside—"or have company." He turned to go, saying, "I will come back another time."

She reached for his elbow and took hold of the heavy fabric of his sleeve. "No, no—please, your reverence. It's time for me to be gettin' up anyway," she lied. "'Tis I who's the one to be apologizin'." She giggled in embarrassment. "That ain't no way to be greetin' a preacherman! I really am awful sorry." She opened the door wider, ushering the minister in. "But you see, your reverence, it's just that I, uh, work so late at night—so I gotta grab my sleep during the day."

"Ah, that is exactly what I have come to speak with you about, my child. Not about your sleeping habits, but about your work." The reverend wandered into the cluttered room and looked about for an empty chair.

Harriett rushed to a tattered old overstuffed wingback and yanked the cast-off clothing from it, jamming the armful into a bureau drawer, thinking, *Oh, please—no sermons. Not at this ungodly hour!*

Cramming the rest of the unmentionables into another drawer, she said, "Please, your reverence, sit yourself down." She motioned to the empty chair. "Make yourself to home, why don't you."

As the slender Lutheran minister sat, Harriett looked

around for her house slippers and stepped into them, as if that would make her somehow more presentable. She reached out and pulled up the window shades, letting the intrusive sunlight stream in. Opening both windows to allow whatever stale odors lingered from the night before to escape, she sat on her bed across from the clergyman and waited, hoping he would not try to save her soul again.

She caught her breath and said casually, "I suppose you're not here to see me professionally, your reverence." She giggled devilishly, an evil little glint in her eye. "So what it is you want, uh, what is it I can do to help you?"

With somber visage, the minister said piously, "It is I who am here to help you, my child—"

Oh, no! she thought. *Here it comes! Damn his holy hide all to hell and back!*

"You are in grave physical danger, my child, and I felt I should warn you." He reached for her hand.

Her dark blue eyes widened, and she pulled away in alarm. This was not what she had expected. Physical danger? "Who? It's that Bart Cranklin, ain't it? Well, I can handle the likes of him, your reverence. I thank you for your worryin', but I'll be takin' care of that sonuv—"

"No, my child." His serious demeanor stern, he took hold of her tiny hand with his long bony fingers and lowered his voice almost to a whisper. "It's the Mad Ripper! You are not safe while he is about, menacing and massacring our fair city's young women."

"Oh, him," she said offhandedly, laughing from relief. "I was afraid you was really on to somethin'." She shook her head and smiled, trying without success to retrieve her hand. "I know it ain't clever to walk out by myself at night, but everybody says that that loon only works in the wharf district. We're all of a couple of miles or more from there. Besides," she said, tossing her black curls, "I ain't

89

helpless. I can take care of myself. Those other girls was just plain careless.''

As the reverend pulled her toward him, his voice pierced her very being. She could feel the heat of his breath as he admonished her. His words were tools, and he used them skillfully—pleading, reasoning, and finally, threatening.

With the same great passion he employed in delivering his sermons, Reverend Bergendorfer laid forth on the subject of sensual sin and the Mad Ripper, all the while bringing the young woman ever closer. He tried to explain how she could cleanse her soul and save her life all at the same time. It had something to do with him. She was almost in his arms, his mesmerizing intonations tugging at her almost as strongly as were his grasping hands.

But Harriett Hartley had stopped listening to the hypnotic drone of the reverend's voice and no longer paid heed to his words. The significance of his initial warning seeped in, and she grew truly frightened for her own safety. She might as well have been alone in the room, she was so deep into her own thoughts. No longer aware of the here and now, her imagination ran wild as she visualized the Mad Ripper chasing her down some dark, deserted street, grabbing her from behind, and slashing her throat.

As she fought back panic, she admitted to herself that Reverend Bergendorfer was right, and she was indeed in danger. After all, she had heard that the newspapers all agreed that the murderer only butchered ladies of the evening. Even if that last girl had been an actress, the slasher had mistaken her for a streetwalker. Harriett realized she had no guarantee that this bloodthirsty madman would restrict himself to the waterfront area. For all she knew, he might be lurking outside her front stoop, just waiting for her to come out so he could slit her throat. Worse yet, he might be right here in her room! How did she know that the slasher might not be the Reverend Bergendorfer?

The thought terrified her, jolting her back to the present. Suddenly aware of the reverend's lips brushing her cheek, Harriett tried to tear herself from the Lutheran minister's grip. But his long bony fingers were strong, and he held on to her arms, pulling her toward him.

All at once he was on his feet, dragging her up with him. His hands on her large breasts, he pushed her back onto her bed and threw himself on top of her, pawing and squeezing her.

"My child, my beautiful child. I must cleanse your soul from within. Only my holy organ can—"

"Reverend!" she cried, rolling over, trying to break free. "Stop! Please!"

He rolled back on top and took her face in his hands. Lunging for her lips, he attempted to kiss her, but she broke loose of his grasp and turned her head quickly. His lips and tongue sank into her ear. The suction was so great that Harriett was unable to hear for a moment. The harder she struggled, the more insistent the minister became. Her resistance seemed to fuel his lust, and he ripped her housecoat open to behold her ripe bosom.

As he took hold of a luscious breast in each hand, Harriett relaxed completely, her body going limp. If he were the Mad Ripper, she would soon be dead. Her head off to one side, her eyes closed tightly, she said with deep feeling through clenched teeth, "Our Father, which art in Heaven, hallowed be Thy name—"

The lecherous preacher stopped in midmouthful.

"—give us this day . . . ." She intoned the Lord's prayer with great emotion.

Reverend Bergendorfer rolled off Harriett and closed her housecoat. As he sat up, he joined her in prayer. ". . . and lead us not into temptation . . ." His head bowed, he stood and pulled her to her feet, still praying. He put her hands together in prayer and held them between his. ". . . for Thine

91

is the kingdom and the power and the glory. Amen." He kissed her gently, reverently on the forehead. "Bless you, my child."

He wasn't the ripper after all. Relief flooded through her. "Oh, thank you, your reverence! Thank you for caring! And thank you for the warning. I'll be eternally grateful, I will!" She turned from him and reached under her bed for her one large battered piece of luggage. "You're right as rain, though, and I figger I am in danger," she said as if nothing untoward had happened. "There's only one thing for me to do—get the hell outta St. Louis just as soon as possible. I'm leavin' right now!"

She slammed the portmanteau down on her bed and unloaded her dresser drawers into it. "Now, if you'd please be excusin' me, your reverence, I'd like to get me clothes on. Me mum is gonna have some surprise when I show up on her doorstep. She thinks I left Chicago for good."

Momentarily shaken by the young woman's unexpected reaction, the reverend stammered and sighed. This was not at all what he had planned, but there was no turning back now. He reluctantly headed for the front door. "You're a wise girl, Harriett. And there's a six o'clock train for Chicago. Of course, if you should change your mind, I will be at the church rectory after I've made the rest of my rounds. Or you can always find me at the mission." He stopped and took her hand in his again, kissing it gently. "When this ghastly threat is over, my child, please come back. Our parish will welcome you warmly. I will welcome you warmly. God be with you, my—"

"Thank you, your reverence," she interrupted. "I am most appreciative of the thought, but I got me a train to catch, and I sure as hell wouldn't wanna miss it."

She watched him go for only a second before shutting the door and returning to her packing. She left what she couldn't fit into her portmanteau and dressed quickly, piling on as many pieces of clothing as she could. She had few really valuable possessions, and her life meant more to her than any tawdry trinkets she might have to leave behind. The ripper posed too much of a threat for her to loiter. She must catch that train for Chicago. What time did the reverend say it left—six o'clock?

At Union Station, Harriett stood at the ticket counter, arguing with the clerk. She wanted an inexpensive Pullman seat, but the clerk informed her that Pullman seats were all sold out. The only accommodation the clerk could offer for the six o'clock to Chicago was a very expensive sleeping compartment. Traffic was brisk, he explained, since the third slashing, and everybody wanted to leave.

"But there ain't no way I can afford—"

"It don't make no difference to me," the clerk said, wiping his nose on the back of his hand, his eyes focused a little to the side of her left ear. "Take the sleeping room or get out of line and let somebody else through."

"It's too much mon—"

"There'll be another train for Chicago—next week. Suit yourself, girlie." He looked over Harriett's shoulder. "Next!"

"No, wait. I might not even be alive in another week." She dug down into her handbag and rummaged until she came up with the exact amount. With her looks, she reasoned, she could always find someone with cash to spend on her services. Possibly even on the train, if she were lucky. She plunked down the money. "Here."

The clerk wiped his nose again and handed her the ticket, then looked past her and barked, "Next!"

Harriett had packed a large meal, and she struggled down the station platform with her big traveling case and the cumbersome food parcel. The train stood in the station, breathing steam. She located the right car, car C, and a conductor helped her up the steps and checked her ticket to make sure she was in the correct place. As he pointed out her compartment, he told her that a porter would be by a little later to make up her bed.

Harriett found her way to the much too expensive compartment 4C. She reasoned that since she had already paid for the ticket, she might as well enjoy the experience. She had never traveled first class before, but if she were going home, she might as well do it in style.

The plush compartment was not as spacious as she had expected for the money, but it would provide her with complete privacy. She dumped her portmanteau and food parcel on the seat and took off her hat and coat and hung them on a large brass hook. She decided that as long as she was by herself, she could make herself as comfortable as she pleased. She removed all her outer clothing, many pieces she had been unable to pack but refused to part with, and then undid her dress and several petticoats.

Glancing out the window, she realized that the train was still in the station, and her privacy would not be complete until the train left and was moving. She lighted the ornate brass lantern hanging on the wall opposite the seat and pulled down the window shade, smiling at her own modesty.

She might as well go all the way, she thought, as she undid her shoes and slipped them off, wriggling her toes luxuriously. She opened her portmanteau, removed her housecoat, and tossed it on the seat beside her. Off came her unmentionables—she loved the feel of air on her naked flesh. She put on her housecoat, leaving it open in front, and placed her large traveling bag on the floor under the window.

Sitting down, she propped up her feet on her suitcase and turned her attention to her meal. She opened the parcel she had so carefully packaged and spread the food out on the wrappings. She was about to bite into a sausage-and-cheese sandwich, when there was a knock at the door.

"Just a minute!" she yelled, putting the lunch parcel together quickly and closing her housecoat. "I'll be right there." Wasn't it a little early for the porter to be making up the bed? she wondered. She pulled the sash tight so her body was fully covered, straightened her hair, and slid open the door a crack.

"Yes?" she said, as she looked in surprise at the tall figure in the doorway. It was definitely not the porter—at least, no porter she had ever seen. Fancy overcoat, very expensive muffler, dapper hat with the brim pulled way down, suede gloves, carrying a bright new carpetbag. No, most assuredly not a porter—more like a really rich gentleman. There was something familiar about this one, but with the muffler up and the brim down, she could barely make out a face.

"Excuse me, miss," said the posh stranger in a husky whisper, "but I couldn't help noticing you from the platform as you got on board. I'm sure you hear this all the time, but you are quite lovely—"

Harriett blinked long black lashes and smiled. "Oh? You really think so? Why, thank you, sir, I'm sure."

"—and I was wondering if you would care for some company on the long journey. I'm sure we could think of something to do to pass the time."

This was what Harriett had hoped for—someone to pay for her trip—but she had already grown accustomed to the idea of the luxury of a little privacy—just for a while, of course.

"Thank you. Maybe later? Right now, I'd like to be relaxin' and spendin' a little time—"

She caught herself up short as a gloved hand opened to display three shiny coins—three very large coins!—enough to pay her way to China!

"Well, now, don't mind if I do," she said, changing her attitude, her voice mellow and flirtatious. "It's a terrible long way to Chicago. I mean, we ain't even out of the station yet, and I'm already gettin' bored." She smiled brightly and accepted the coins, turning them over, examining them carefully. She motioned the customer in and slid the door closed behind her, locking it.

"We might as well get acquainted, darlin'," she said seductively. "I'm Harriett—and what would I be callin' you?"

"'Darlin'' is fine with me."

Harriett knew the type, the kind who hedged because he was probably married and afraid of trouble later. "All right, darlin'. But why don't you be gettin' yourself unbundled and relaxed." She turned and reached for her sandwich. "Hungry? Want to share a sandwich? Sausage and cheese—there's plenty here for the both of us. I even brung some wine." She held up a large corked bottle half-full of a deep red fluid. "Wanna sip?"

"Perhaps later. A little something to eat would be nice after we, uh, get better acquainted—"

Don't waste much time, does he? she thought, waiting for him to take off his hat and coat. She realized that the three coins were enough to pay for her services from St. Louis to Chicago and back; so whatever the gentleman wanted, she would give him—within reason, of course.

"Turn around and don't look," the fancy stranger said, taking Harriett firmly by the shoulders and turning her away. "I prefer to undress without an audience."

He's shy! she said to herself. *Now, that is sweet.* "Of course, darlin'," she said. "Anything you say." She dropped her housecoat and sat naked on the seat with her back to her coy customer, waiting. From the sound of it, she could tell this gentleman was the neat type. As each garment came off, she could hear it being folded.

While she sat there listening, Harriett wondered if he was overly modest because he was too small and was ashamed— or was he afraid of scaring her because he was too large? She would soon find out, since there could not be many more garments to take off.

She heard the clasps of the large carpetbag clicking open. Her curiosity getting the best of her, she started to turn around.

"Don't turn yet," came the husky whisper from behind her. "The fun's about to begin."

Harriett shuddered in anticipation and couldn't resist one short glimpse. She turned her head very quickly—and as her dark blue eyes saw what it was her customer wanted to conceal, she opened her mouth to scream. But the scream never came.

The murderer wrenched Harriett's head roughly toward the window, and abruptly ended her life.

Wiping the scalpel clean on Harriett's housecoat, the murderer carefully sidestepped a large puddle of slippery blood and reached into the big carpetbag, took out moistened cloths wrapped in waxed paper, and a large corked whiskey bottle filled with water, and meticulously bathed off every telltale spot of blood before dressing.

Stripping naked before slitting each sporting girl's throat had been a stroke of pure genius, the slasher reflected proudly with an air of invincibility. Not a trace of blood to track down, not a shred of a clue left behind for those imbeciles from the police department to trace. With one final gesture of sangfroid, the slasher sat down on the un-soiled section of the seat and bit into the part of the sandwich not sopped with blood, washing it down with the murdered woman's wine. Might as well relax and enjoy the rewards of a job well done.

The train had not yet left the station, and if all went as it should, the corridor would be clear, and the body might not be discovered until it reached Chicago. As the last mouthful of sandwich was washed down with a large gulp of wine, there was a knock at the door. The murderer froze, not daring to breathe.

When the stout porter heard no response from 4C, he knocked again. He knew the compartment was occupied, because he had noticed the shapely young woman enter it. He had admired the curve of her body, the cut of her clothes. He looked forward to being in the compartment with her, drinking in her delicious scent from close up.

After the second knock the porter called out, but there was still no response. His first reaction was to go on to 5C, but he wanted to get every last tip he could, so he tried the handle, knocking and calling as he did.

The slasher pressed up against the locked door, calling out softly, "Later, please. I'm a mess right now."

The porter persisted. "But I should make up your bed, ma'am. I gets off at Litchfield, and I wants to have all the beds made up afore I changes trains."

"I said later!"

Chapter 10

Captain Curtis Bernard rushed through Union Station with Jessica Starbuck and Ki close on his heels. The trio climbed on to the six o'clock for Chicago, which had been held at the depot. The body of the fourth slasher victim had been discovered, and policemen were everywhere.

After viewing the murder scene, the trio spoke with the conductor. But he knew nothing beyond having directed the young woman to her compartment. He never saw her again. The police officer first at the scene reported that the victim had been identified as Harriett Hartley, another of the city's many ladies of the evening.

The three turned their attention to the porter who found the body. The badly shaken man, his normally dark complexion an ashen gray, sat on the steps of sleeping car C and, with a shaking hand, wiped vomit from his lips into a crumpled handkerchief.

"The conductor tells me your name is Horace Washington," Captain Bernard said. "Do you think you're up to speaking with us yet?"

The porter looked up blankly.

"We need to ask you some questions. I know how you feel, but it's necessary."

Slowly the porter shook his head, then changing his mind, he nodded.

"Could you tell us exactly what happened?" the chief

of detectives asked gently, his crystal-blue eyes softening, his rugged smile understanding.

Ignoring Jessica and Ki, Horace Washington focused all his attention on the captain. It would be too much effort to handle three people—one friendly policeman was all he could take right now. Sensing this, Jessie and Ki faded back, blending in with the milling travelers, listening from a respectful distance.

"Take your time, Horace," the captain urged. "There's no hurry." He was stretching the truth. He knew that without the porter's information, they could not proceed. The man's story was vital, and the sooner they heard it, the more chance they'd have of catching the slasher. But pressing the man would only delay matters, since he might freeze up and refuse to speak. "Just begin wherever you want, Horace."

"Thank you, Cap'n. I appreciates." The porter smiled wanly and stuffed the foul-smelling handkerchief into a back trouser pocket. "I found her—" His eyes started to cross, and he looked as if he might pass out at any moment.

"Easy now, Horace. Just relax and take a deep breath. Let's go back to when you first went to car C. What were you doing?"

"Well, sir, I was jes' fixin' up all the beds early." A sliver of a smile turned up the sides of his now pale thick lips. "You see, folks what kin afford fancy sleeping 'partments kin sometimes be kinda free with their money." He waited for Captain Bernard to acknowledge his statement, staring hard into the blue eyes.

The captain nodded patiently and waited, keeping total eye contact.

"Most times, I kin make real good tips iffen I do a little bit extra. And cuz I gotta change trains at Litchfield, I figgers I best start makin' up the beds quick as lightnin', afore we leaves the station. The more beds I makes up by the time we gets to Litchfield, the more tips—you gets my meanin'?''

"Yes, of course. Makes perfect sense."

"Well, sir, I gits all the way through car A and car B, and I starts on C. That's where we is now." He pointed up to the big C in the window of the car. "I done three C, and when I gits to four C, I knocks like I allus does, but at first nobody answers. Most times, when folks ain't in their 'part-ment, I jes' lets myself in with the passkey and makes up the beds. Figger I kin come back later to see iffen there's anythin' else they's wantin'." Again, he stopped and stared at the captain, waiting.

"Very clever."

"Yessir, it works jes' fine," he said proudly. "Well, sir, like I said, when I gits to four C and there's no answer, I tries again, cuz I seen the lady come onboard. Soon's I tries the handle, she says, ever so softly, for me to come back later."

"Are you certain it was Miss Hartley's voice you heard? It was through a door. Was it a man's voice—or a woman's? Think hard."

"I think it was a woman, but I couldn't swear. I don't know. I never gave it no mind. I never did gets to talk to her afore this, so how would I know what she sounds like?" His big brown eyes clouded up, and he faltered, remembering the scene.

"That's good, Horace. You're doing fine. Now, take a deep breath again and tell me exactly what the voice said, as best you recall."

"Truth is, sir, it's all jes' about knocked clean outta my head." He sucked in air and held it. Letting it out slowly, he continued. "Let's see—I tells her I wants to make up her bed. She says sumpthin' about being a mess and I should come back later." He snapped his fingers. "That's right! I 'member thinkin' to myself that she were much too pretty

101

to ever be no mess." His face went ashen again as he relived the moment he discovered her body.

"Come on, Horace. Breathe deep."

The porter shut his eyes tightly for two deep breaths and rushed on, hoping to get the ordeal over with in a hurry. "I takes the lady at her word, and heads for five C. The folks in five C is out, so I goes in and makes up the beds. While I'm workin' on it, I hears the door to four C slide open and then slide closed. It were real soft-like, but I been listenin' jes' in case the pretty lady wants me to come back. Well, when I hears that, I figgers that the pretty lady's gone for some air. So when I finishes with five C, I goes back to four C, and, and—"

"Is that it? Is there any more?"

Horace Washington shook his head sadly and gulped.

Captain Bernard patted the unnerved porter on the shoulder, thanked him, and told him he could leave. Before the captain could speak again, the stout porter had bolted and was gone.

Jessica approached, with Ki behind her. "We heard everything," she said. "Sounds as if he caught the slasher at work. Lucky for the porter he didn't barge on in or he'd be dead, too."

Ki nodded agreement. "This madman is growing increasingly bold."

The trio climbed back on the train, returning to compartment 4C for a more thorough examination.

The captain frowned and shook his head as he surveyed the grisly scene once again. "We're not one step closer than we were after the third slashing."

"Oh, yes, we are," Jessica said. "From the evidence the slasher left behind, we know he's completely insane." She pointed to the partially eaten sandwich. "There's blood on half that sandwich—and finger marks on the blood-soaked half! No one in his right mind would have the stomach to eat after doing such a thing." She raised an eyebrow. "Of course, no one in his right mind would go around mutilating people in the first place."

Ki said, "And bathing after each slashing. From the looks of this, he must have been drenched in blood. He knows he'll be stopped if he goes out with blood all over him, so he took the precaution of washing it off." He looked at Captain Bernard, then Jessica, and picked up one of the strips of wet, pink-stained muslin from the floor. "These bloody cloths he left behind show he came prepared."

"Unless they're the victim's," Captain Bernard said.

Jessie shook her head. "Look around. There are more garments here than would fit into one portmanteau. She obviously wore several layers of clothing. If she was so cramped for space, why would she pack strips of muslin? It makes no sense."

The three climbed off the train again, breathing deeply, ridding their lungs of the stench of death.

"Besides," Jessie added, "the murderer couldn't take a chance on getting stopped with those bloody cloths in his satchel—or whatever he was carrying—so he had to leave them behind."

Ki said, "Going on the assumption that the slasher avoids drenching his clothes in blood by undressing before killing his victims, did he choose ladies of the evening because he could undress in their presence without calling attention— or are ladies of the evening his target?"

Captain Bernard motioned to the policeman standing guard over car C. Answering Ki, he said, "We won't know that until we catch him." To the policeman, "Any witnesses?"

"Yes, sir." The stocky young policeman pointed to a hunchbacked old peddlerwoman standing off to the side, a basket of wares hanging from around her scrawny neck. "She claims she saw somebody suspicious leaving the train just before the alarm went up. But the old biddy may be looking for attention or a handout.''

The captain approached the old crone, his most congenial smile showing blue-white teeth. "Hello, mother. The policeman here tells me you saw something.''

"Well, mebbe I did and mebbe I didn't.'' She squinted up at him, baring her toothless gums. "But I ain't makin' no money standin' around jawin'.''

He resisted the urge to step back from her fetid breath. Instead, he held his ground and reached into his pocket. Dropping some coins on her tray, he asked, "This take care of it?''

She cackled. "Yep.'' Her tiny black eyes glistened as she described the "real gent'' she had seen getting off the train. She noticed him, she said, because he wore his hat brim pulled way down and his muffler pulled up to cover most of his face. She thought it odd at the time for someone indoors to be so covered up, especially since the station's Grand Hall was always very warm. She particularly admired the new oversized carpetbag he carried.

The chief of detectives relaxed his smile. "Is that all? Just someone who looked too warm?''

The crone eyed Captain Bernard, sizing him up, and finally said, "You won't run me in iffen I tell you somethin' else—somethin' real peculiar?''

"Please continue. You won't be arrested.''

"It'll cost more.'' She grinned and waited.

The captain dropped another coin on her tray.

The old peddlerwoman pocketed the coin and sidled closer to him, until her breath nearly choked him, and said, "I tried to pick his pockets—you know, bumpin' him with me tray like I always—'' She paused and grinned. "Well, sir, I tried both sides—but he ain't got no wallet nowheres. I got the best hands in this here depot, and I'm here to tell ya', he weren't carryin' nothin'!''

The captain's eyebrows went up.

"That's right." She was pleased at his reaction. "He mighta been dressed up all posh, but his pockets was empty. Don't make no sense."

The chief of detectives thanked the hag and looked at Jessica and Ki. Another strange piece of a very curious puzzle.

Reverend Bergendorfer made the rounds of the "soiled doves" residing in the mission's neighborhood. He brought salvation to a soul or two, and a great deal of pleasure to himself, both physically and spiritually. He was driven, a man with a purpose, and he cleansed as many soiled doves as he could. His stamina buckled after the first few days, and he rested before pushing on.

The entire city had been locked in the grip of terror after the third slashing, and few people strayed from their homes alone. Groups passed by with clubs and bricks, heading for a confrontation with some suspect or other. But Reverend Bergendorfer's Lutheran tunic, collar, and Bible were his passport through vigilante lines. No one stopped him or gave him a second glance.

The sun slowly dipped behind the buildings across the street, and the minister knew he would have to return to the mission soon. It was no longer safe for anyone to be out at night, and the police chief had ordered a curfew. Anyone without the proper credentials caught on the streets after seven o'clock at night would be arrested and hauled in for questioning. The possibility of a vigilante lynching loomed high in everyone's fears.

Reverend Bergendorfer had one more stop to make before curfew—little Susie Gallichotte, who lived two doors down. The minister hurried up the steps and knocked on her door. He knew she had no customer, because she always put a sign in her window when she entertained a client. That way no one would disturb her. The reverend thought he heard a scuffle from inside, but he could not be certain. The lights were on, so she must be home. There was no answer, so he knocked again, a little harder.

"Susie, my child, it is Reverend Bergendorfer. Please open the door."

He heard someone moving around inside, but the drapes were drawn, so he could not see in. He knocked again, more emphatically. She had dodged him before, but he knew that with no sign showing, she was available.

"I know you are in there, Susie—I can hear you. I do not leave until we have had a little, uh, chat. Now, be a good child and open this door."

Someone approached the door, and a husky whisper from the other side said, "Go away—I'm busy! Please leave! I have a customer."

A crooked smile split the preacher's gaunt face. He laughed and said, "Oh, no you don't, my child. You cannot fool Arthur Bergendorfer." He pounded on the door. "Let me in. I know you are alone—you have not put your sign in the window." He pleaded. "Listen to me, my child, I must see you now. It is not very nice to keep people waiting on the stoop this way."

"I forgot the sign," came the insistent whisper. "Please go away!"

"I will not. You never forget your sign. With God as my witness, I know you are alone. It is urgent that I see you. I must speak with you now. I promise you, I will not leave until you see me. I will stay on your stoop all night if need be." His voice softened, pleading again. "You will not regret it, my child. Open the door."

He heard the bolt being turned, and he grinned broadly, his slender face a mass of creases. He backed up and fastidiously straightened his tunic as he waited for the door to

106

be unlocked. When it opened, he stepped inside, his pulse racing in anticipation, a full-blown erection preceding him into the house.

"Susie, my child," he said playfully, "I have something for you."

The front door closed as he entered the parlor, and Reverend Bergendorfer caught sight of Susie Gallichotte's naked body sprawled in the doorway to the bedroom.

From behind him, he heard, "And I have something for you!"

The slicing scalpel hurt only for a moment.

Chapter 11

Mayor Donnally Palmer stood glowering at Hiram Carstairs and Curtis Bernard, beads of sweat trickling off his glistening baldness into his collar. The stocky little man pulled himself up to his full five feet four inches and gnawed on his stogie. His stubby fingers drumming on his checkered vest, thumbs hooked into ornate suspenders, he finished his tirade.

"If I go down, I haul you two bastards with me! How do you think the public's gonna react when they hear about the fourth slashing?" His dark eyes bulged as he glared across his big oak desk at the chief of police and the chief of detectives.

Chief Carstairs smirked uncomfortably and said to Captain Bernard, "Wanna bet the commissioner's on his neck?"

The captain looked straight ahead, ignoring the chief's attempt at comic relief.

"Damn it all to hell, Hi—be serious! This Mad Ripper thing has gone far enough! You two gotta make an arrest, and fast! And what the hell you doin' with your damn dog here? Are you insane, bringing that flea-bitten hound to city hall? It's bad enough, you bring him to work. Police headquarters is no place fer a hound—you know that!"

Hiram Carstairs reached down protectively to scratch Archie behind the ears. The hound looked up, panting appreciatively, his tail flopping noisily against his master's pantleg.

"Damn it all, Hi—keep that hound at home! It doesn't look right, you takin' that mutt everywhere you go."

"Archie's no mutt, and you know it!" Chief Carstairs's voice was defensive, yet tinged with guilt. "Don, you know me better'n that. You know I'd never keep Archie with me without a good reason."

Mayor Palmer did know. Chief Carstairs had told everyone at headquarters about the shooting of his hounds—murder, he'd called it. A man had secretly been assigned to keep an eye on Chief Carstairs—one the department could hardly afford, considering the hysteria over the slasher crisis. But Mayor Palmer, Captain Bernard, and most of the force agreed that the chief might be in danger. And the chief didn't have to know about the protective tail.

The mayor nodded, and the police chief understood that tensions were building with so many deaths and so few clues. Archie seemed a good target for the mayor's pent-up emotions. Now he had added guilt to those emotions, tantamount to kicking the dog.

Mayor Palmer relented on the chief and his dog, and turned toward Captain Bernard. "Well, what good are that woman and her Oriental friend? Damn it all to hell, Curt, I'm surprised at you—you gonna let a girl and a Chinaman solve this case for you?"

"He's Japanese, if that matters—and half-white. And if you live long enough to make it to the next election, Mr. Mayor, I'm voting you out." He laughed. "That is, if I'm still around then myself." He sobered. "Jessica Starbuck and Ki's reputations are as solid as they come, Mr. Mayor. And they can make progress where the police are shut out."

"You may be right."

"I know I am. We can use their help—hell, at this point, we can use all the help we can get!"

"If you say so." Ashes from the stogie dropped on the mayor's huge belly; one snap of his suspenders dislodged them. "You know, the police commissioner is breathing down my neck. He wants the two of you out." His big eyes raked both men. "Says you're not doing your jobs or the slasher would already be at the end of a rope."

Chief Carstairs growled, "Then let *him* find that carving lunatic." He wished he had his pipe with him. "Hell and damnation, Don—we're doing everything we can! You know that! I gave the word again to bring in all the people connected in any way with knives and razors. If that don't stop the slashings, if we don't have the ripper in our jails, then I don't know what we can do." He shrugged.

"But why," the mayor asked, "did you have to let that damn fool Clark Buttrick go? He and his vicious band of vigilantes will demolish this city when they hear of the fourth slashing. Your timing's rotten, Hi."

"His wife and kids put up bail. What could I do? And what was the judge thinking—setting bail at all? If I had my way, I'd lock him up and throw away the key. Never did like that insufferable bastard."

The mayor's eyes pleaded as he asked Captain Bernard the question he already had answers to: "You got *any* clues, anything you can hang your hat on?" The stocky little mayor threw his hands up without waiting to hear what the captain might say, and chuckled wryly. "I know—you'd have told me if you had. God, I feel so helpless!"

Captain Bernard shook his head. "You're not alone. We all do, Mr. Mayor."

Hiram Carstairs grunted.

Archie yawned loudly.

As Jessica Starbuck and Ki walked toward the Red Fox Saloon, several of the half-drunk toughs standing out front commented and elbowed one another. Three thugs—one

111

with big ears, one with a huge belly, and one with two front teeth missing—growled and took a step back. These men had seen much in their time, but few had seen a gorgeous honey-blonde in tight jeans and a tighter shirt—packing a six-shooter. Not in the city, anyway.

Jessie and Ki had to pass the tavern to get to their destination, and the last time they did so, three of the ruffians had tried to stop them, much to the men's regret. Ki had dispatched them barehanded, which they would not soon forget. They retreated now in deference to Ki's special abilities, but they eyed Jessica.

Drawing their bravery from a bottle and their numbers, the three men waited until Ki and Jessie were parallel; then they swooped down on Ki. Big Ears grabbed Ki's arms from behind as Toothless grabbed his feet, and Ki felt himself being jerked off the ground. The man with the huge belly made a lunge for the honey-blonde, but she sidestepped his grasp and drew her weapon.

"Put him down!" Jessie's large green eyes blazed at Ki's helplessness. "You heard me. Now put him down slowly, before I really get angry and do something you won't like." She pulled back the hammer on the revolver and waited.

The men, brazen with beer, laughed. Big Ears and Toothless raised Ki even higher, until the struggling Asian was almost at shoulder height. The fat bully reached for the gun jutting out from his belt, his beefy hand clasping the battered butt.

"Didn't your daddy tell you never to play with guns, little girl?" His revolver had almost cleared his belt as he mocked her. "You could get hurt, blondie—or, worse, you might hurt somebody else." His gun out, he leveled it at her, his voice brittle. "Now put your toy away and you won't get shot."

Jessica squeezed the trigger and fired, and the large man spun around, grabbing his shoulder and howling in pain.

His arm went limp, the revolver dangling from a useless hand. She pointed her six-shooter first at Toothless and then at Big Ears.

"As I was saying, gentlemen, please put my friend down gently."

The two toughs complied, lowering Ki to a standing position and backing away. One of the onlookers, no longer smiling, reached for his revolver, but Ki's hand chopped down on the man's wrist with such force the snap of bones could be heard ten feet away.

Jessica kept the drunken group covered until she and Ki could get by and on their way. In disgust, they jogged the rest of the way, upset with themselves for wasting so much time.

"Next time," Ki said as they reached the steps of the small red-brick house, "let's approach from the other end of the street and avoid those drunks. We don't have time to play their games."

Jessie smiled as she knocked on the front door. She and Ki stood on the stoop and waited until Priscilla Whitaker peered through the living room curtains and then unlocked the front door. Almost before the door swung open, the two were through it and into the poorly lighted parlor.

Ki said, "There's been another slashing. If you have any idea where Dr. Whitaker is, please let us know. We must find him fast—he's in danger."

"Yes," Jessie added with concern. "If you care anything about your former husband, please tell us where he is. At this point, with four murders, the public is going to start hanging people who even look like they might not have an alibi. People are already becoming irrational. This should push them to hysteria."

Her fine dark brown hair pulled straight back and knotted at the nape of her neck, Priscilla Whitaker stood tall and proud. As Ki and Jessie continued, she faltered slightly.

113

Her magnificent bearing, remarkable posture, and ladylike demeanor bespoke better times. A high-ruffled collar covered a regal neck, and her tiny waistline obviously needed no corsets. Her grace and dignity added an air of near-beauty to her almost plain features.

"Why in heaven's name would you think I know of Louis's whereabouts? The first time you were here, I thought I had assured you I knew nothing of him. We are no longer married, you know."

"Yes," Jessie said. "But if you tried so hard to get him released on bail, you would more than likely continue to work on his behalf after he'd been freed."

Ki added, "It's logical. And we've looked everywhere for him."

"We must find him. He's in extreme danger." Jessica's eyes searched the room for clues to their client's whereabouts. "Once the newspapers let the world know there's been a fourth brutal murder, no surgeon will be safe—and the police have already proved Dr. Whitaker was involved with the first two victims." She stared into the woman's thick-lidded eyes, looking for a hint.

"I don't want him hanged!" Priscilla said. "He didn't do anything. If you take him back to jail, they'll try to lynch him, I just know it!"

"Not if we hide him, they won't." Jessica argued. "He isn't safe here. If we thought to look here, so will others—and they won't be so polite."

Priscilla relented. "You may be right. But how will you get him to your hiding place?" She glanced toward the stairs to the basement. "At least here, I know where he is—and so far, he's been safe."

Ki smiled. "We will wait until dark to move him. Just before curfew, the four of us will walk out of here as if two couples out on the town. Jessica will be on his arm—she

114

can better protect him; you will be with me, if you don't mind.''

The slender woman shook her head, looking up slightly at Ki. "It's too risky. I'm afraid for him."

From the basement stairwell, a deep voice said, "It's my only chance, Sissie. If Jessica and Ki are right, a vigilante mob should be here at any time." Louis Whitaker emerged from the doorway to the basement and stood facing them, a dark stubble on his jaw drawing attention away from his magnificent mustache.

"Not just the vigilantes," Ki said soberly. "The police are rounding up every surgeon, butcher, barber, and veterinarian again. Pressure from the mayor and the police commissioner is forcing their hand."

Jessica nodded. "This time they want to make sure they find the right man. Unfortunately, with the public terrified, even the jails won't be safe." She looked at Dr. Whitaker and smiled. "My father would want us to do everything we could to protect you. And that does not mean handing you over to the police." She moved toward Priscilla. "If I could borrow a gown—my attire is not appropriate for two couples out on the town."

Ki added, "And you better get shaved, Doctor."

While the surgeon freshened up, Priscilla led Jessie to her bedroom and went through her wardrobe, looking for an appropriate outfit. After several minutes of picking and choosing, she selected the right frock that would fit over jeans and shirt. An elbow-length cape covered any questionable bulges, and a matching drawstring handbag proved just the right size to conceal Jessica's six-shooter.

The four headed toward the front door, when Ki raised a hand for them to stop. "Shhh! I hear something." He waved the others back while he peered down the street in both directions. He suddenly motioned for everyone to get way back. In the dusky shadows cast by the glow of gaslight, he saw a chilling sight.

Marching six or eight abreast, more than two dozen men—a noisy vigilante mob—strode down the street toward them. Some carried lighted torches, others held clubs or other makeshift weapons. Some had guns holstered, a few brandished rifles and shotguns. One man had the noose.

The men spilled onto the sidewalks on both sides of the street, and they seemed to be heading toward Priscilla Whitaker's house.

At the head of the pack was a familiar face—Clark Buttrick.

Chapter 12

Clark Buttrick swaggered as he marched, leading his band of vigilantes self-righteously into battle. He had heard of the fourth slashing even before the newspapers proclaimed the terrible deed. He and his group of toughs planned to get the jump on everyone else. After drinking their fill at the Rusty Nail Saloon, they had taken up their torches and gone out after the Mad Ripper. Stopping to wet their whistles at every saloon they came to, they had finally chanced on the Red Fox Saloon.

The man with big ears and the man with two front teeth missing, brothers under the skin, had asked to join the crowd. In return for the privilege they described the blonde and the Oriental they had encountered. While their story contained gross exaggeration, it sounded familiar. The men who had been at police headquarters when Buttrick and two of his men faced Jessica and Ki, recognized the descriptions and the actions.

"They're part of this!" Buttrick cried. "They're the ones who're hiding that sonuvabitch Whitaker. And we all know Whitaker's the Mad Ripper!"

The boozed-up crowd yelled agreement. The many beers and whiskeys had blinded their reason, and they were ready to string someone up. It mattered little who they hanged. The men wanted violence, and they wanted it now. Buttrick, sensitive to his mob's appetite for vengeance, had fomented the men further. He taunted and encouraged them.

"Follow me, men—these guys say Whitaker's right down the street. We got him this time! And that goddamn blond whore and her chink boyfriend. Come on, men—let's get 'em!"

Buttrick had bolted out the saloon door, Big Ears and Toothless showing him the way to Priscilla Whitaker's house. Spilling off the middle of the street onto the sidewalks, the gang of drunken hoodlums had gained momentum as they struggled to keep up with their beefy leader. This was going to be a night to remember. Clark Buttrick knew the newspapers would make a hero of him for ridding St. Louis of the dreaded ripper. He hoped the papers would take his picture and spell his name right. He would be famous—and rich. That reward would be his!

The entire crowd from the Red Fox Saloon followed the vigilante mob into the street. Excitement was high, and they would all wreak vengeance—especially those humiliated by that Oriental and that girl. Big Ears showed the way, with Toothless right behind. As they approached the house, both men pointed at the little red brick structure.

Dramatically, Buttrick held up a hand to halt his mob. This was a time to grandstand, so he motioned for everyone to stay where he was, while he marched up to the stoop, torch held high. He picked up a loose piece of a brick and hurled it through the front window. Glass shattered, and someone inside cried out.

"Come out, Whitaker! We know you're in there! Come out, you murdering coward!" Buttrick brandished the torch, looking back to his men. "Come on—let's get 'em!" He waved the drunken toughs onward as if leading crusaders against the pagans.

From inside the little house, a gun barked through the broken window; the man next to Buttrick dropped his torch, his body spinning backward. Another shot cracked in the night air, and Big Ears yelped and sank to his knees, a bloody hole in his shoulder.

Buttrick had not counted on resistance. How many of them were there in that house? There had to be at least two—one with a rifle and one with a revolver. He looked around. His men were scattering, some openly fleeing, others jumping for cover. The massive bruiser stood with feet firmly planted, refusing to move an inch. He yanked at his gun butt, trying to pull the six-shooter from the holster; but something sharp zinged out from the broken window and sliced into his arm. With a howl of rage, he stumbled to his right, holding his badly gashed arm. Somebody had thrown a knife at him—at least, it felt like one. Pure hatred blazed from Buttrick's bloodshot eyes.

"Shoot, damn it—shoot!" he called to his men. "Get those sonsuvbitches!"

Several of the toughs who had already drawn their weapons let loose with a volley, blasting the front-room curtains into shreds. Some men fired into the front door, others aimed at the big glassless window, hoping to hit those inside.

Jessica and Ki, who had made sure the Whitakers stayed safely hidden from stray bullets in the basement stairwell, positioned themselves on either side of the big front window. Jessie had her Colt revolver and plenty of ammunition, and Ki had borrowed Priscilla's Winchester after using his only *shuriken* on Clark Buttrick.

From either side of the big window, Jessie and Ki took careful aim, creating a crossfire and making each bullet count. Their object was not to kill, but to fend off the gang of drunken vigilantes. If some died in the process, it would be no great loss.

Priscilla huddled in Louis Whitaker's arms as Jessica and Ki fired round after round at the crowd of toughs. The surgeon noted that at each crack of the rifle, his ex-wife shuddered violently. But the revolver shots came less frequently, as Jessica took longer to fire. There were fewer targets to shoot at.

Ki raised his hand to Jessie, and she stopped firing. The two waited, listening. No one outside returned fire. It was quiet on the street. By the gaslamps along the sidewalks, they could see shadows, most of them moving away from the house. Ki tossed his Winchester to Jessica and motioned his intentions—he would make his way out through the back door and around to the house next door. Jessie knew he wanted to check on the situation without drawing fire.

Ki slipped silently out the back door, hopped the fence into the next yard, and rounded the far corner of the house next door to Priscilla Whitaker's. He hugged the side of the house and peered out from behind a tall bush; he could see the street. Two men lay slumped in the gutter, motionless. Several toughs hobbled off toward the Red Fox Saloon, bloodied and wounded. Only a few remained. But Clark Buttrick was nowhere to be seen. His torch lay sputtering on the sidewalk, and a trail of blood led off down the street.

Two stubborn toughs brought their six-shooters up again, reloaded and ready to continue. Ki sprang out of the bushes with the agility of a cat, delivering a *tobi-geri* kick to the closer of the two gunmen. Ki's heel sent the revolver sailing, and the crunch of the man's wrist snapping could be heard inside the house.

Ki spun quickly, keeping the other gunman in sight through the corner of his eye. He snap-kicked the six-shooter from the second thug and rammed a *nakadata* blow to the man's heart. The vigilante slumped to the street.

A third hoodlum raised a huge Bowie knife and came at Ki. Swiftly effecting a *gedan-barai* block, Ki stopped the thrust in midair. Hacking away at Ki again, the drunken vigilante tried to slit the *te* master's abdomen, but his wrists froze in Ki's viselike grip. One sharp kick to the groin, and

120

the tough sagged to the ground. A short kick to the chin sealed the man's fate.

As Jessie fired over the retreating vigilantes' heads with the Winchester, Ki returned to the house, retracing his steps. He reported his findings. The coast appeared clear, but things could change at any moment. And Clark Buttrick had escaped.

The house would be watched, Jessie and Ki were certain of that; so if they were to get Louis Whitaker away, they would have to use the back door. Priscilla insisted on staying behind, since she wanted to protect her belongings. She kept the Winchester, vowing to use it if any of the vigilante group returned.

As if on cue, there was a loud knock at the front door a matter of moments after Jessica and Ki rushed Dr. Whitaker out. Priscilla gritted her teeth and braced herself for a fight. She would stand them off for as long as the ammunition held out.

"Mrs. Whitaker!" a voice called out. "Are you all right?" The knock grew louder. "Is anybody there? It's Sergeant Hobbs, Mrs. Whitaker."

Priscilla poked her head through the shredded curtains to see the large frame of the neighborhood beat policeman at her front door. With a sigh of relief, she stepped over the debris and opened the door.

"Thank goodness you're here!" she cried. "There were dozens of them! They were drunk, and they insisted I was harboring my ex-husband. That fourth slashing made them crazy, I guess."

"How did you know about a fourth slashing?" the sergeant asked. "The newspapers ain't come out with the news yet." He stared into Priscilla's dark eyes questioningly. "How did you know, ma'am?"

With a slight flutter of her eyelids, she caught herself and took a deep breath. "The crowd shouted it. They knew,

121

and they thought my husband was hiding here. They accused me of harboring him and demanded I hand him over." She looked around at her front room—broken glass and debris everywhere. "They must have come directly from the train station. Those drunken thugs nearly demolished my home, and they deliberately tried to kill me!"

Sergeant Hobbs looked inside, then glanced back at the street, smiling. "Are you alone, ma'am? You didn't do all this by yourself, did you?" He waved a large hand at the slumped bodies in the street.

Priscilla Whitaker held the Winchester in front of her and looked around. Smiling back at the policeman, her eyes wide with innocence, she said wryly, "Do you see anyone else here, Sergeant?"

Jessica and Ki, with Louis Whitaker between them, made their way to the docks a few blocks away. They had not had a chance to prepare a plan before the vigilante group had taken them by surprise. They were now out after curfew, and danger from the police as well as vigilantes menaced them in the darkness.

Ki found a large empty warehouse for them to hide in while they plotted their next move. There was little they could do for the night, but they had to protect Dr. Whitaker at all costs. They sank down on large pieces of burlap and curled up against the chill night air. The strong odor of rotting fish and creosote assaulted their nostrils as they faced one another.

Ki opened his mouth to speak, but Jessica snapped her fingers. "I have an idea! There's only one place I know of where no one will ever think of looking for the doctor— Captain Bernard's rooms!"

Ki said, "But where does he live? And wouldn't he turn the doctor in?"

Jessie shook her head. "I doubt that he'd be in a hurry

to take the doctor in—not after what happened to us just now." She smiled and felt a blush rise in her cheeks. "He lives well south of here—not far off the river at the foot of Grand Boulevard. He gave me the address"—she cleared her throat, relieved that the darkness covered her reddened cheeks—"just in case I needed him for some emergency or other."

Dr. Whitaker, unable to keep silent any longer, said, "This is definitely an emergency. If you think you can trust him, that is." He had not forgotten the captain's brutal interrogation.

"Our problem," Jessie said, "is not whether we can trust the captain, but how in heaven's name we'll get you there. With curfew the streets are much too empty. We'll be noticed the moment we leave here. Ki and I are accustomed to eluding people, but you, Doctor—"

Ki said defensively, "If Jessie says the captain's all right, then he's all right. But where is the foot of Grand Boulevard from here?"

Jessica responded, "It's some distance south of here, down on the other side of town, from what Curt, uh, the captain tells me."

The surgeon said, "Grand Boulevard runs parallel to the river for most of its length; but at the foot, it takes a turn eastward and meets the river. I'd say it's about two miles due south. I know where it is."

"If we took city streets, we would stand out like warts on a peach," Ki observed, wracking his brain for a means of getting the surgeon there safely without being spotted by the police.

"If only we could take a taxicab," the surgeon bemoaned, a sense of defeat in his voice.

Ki smiled, his white teeth catching the rising moonlight from the warehouse window. "Next best thing—let's borrow a boat. Since the captain's place is downriver from

123

here, it would be easy enough to slip into something tied up along the river and float our way down to the foot of Grand.'' He got up and went to the warehouse opening on the river's edge and looked out.

Jessica and Dr. Whitaker followed, both peering out onto the water, straining their eyes in the darkness. Shadows from the three-quarter moon played tricks on the eyes, and what looked like a small rowboat might be pilings casting shadows. Ki slipped silently down to the water's edge, listening.

Not far from where they stood, a small flat-bottom boat rocked against its mooring. Ki located it and called out in a whisper for Jessica and the surgeon to join him. The boat was just large enough for the three of them, but there were no oars. Ki searched the dock area for a length of wood, and finally found a broken plank he could use as both oar and rudder.

The three climbed into the small skiff, and Ki untied the mooring and pushed off. The rapid current of the Mississippi River pulled the fragile craft downstream as a leaf in a storm. Keeping away from open water, Ki maneuvered the boat as close to the shoreline as possible.

''Do you think you can tell when we've come to Grand Boulevard?'' Ki asked the surgeon.

''It's terribly dark, even with the moon, but I can try. If I remember correctly, there's a fur-trading warehouse there at the foot of Grand. You can tell it from the others by the exaggerated overhanging eaves. Even if we don't see the sign, we can't miss the eaves.''

As they bobbed down the length of the town, Dr. Whitaker kept an eye out for the familiar landmark. When he sighted the fur traders' warehouse, he called out softly, and Ki dug the plank into the water as a brake and headed the little boat toward the pier.

The surgeon had been correct, and when they made their

way up the rickety steps to the street, they found themselves at the foot of Grand Boulevard. Captain Bernard's rooms should be less than two blocks away. Ki guided them along the backyards of houses, over fences, and through high brush, avoiding dogs and keeping as far away from the street as possible.

When they located the proper building, Ki stepped up to the door and rapped quietly. Jessica and the surgeon waited in the shadows. On the second knock they heard someone moving about inside. As they watched, a lamp glowed to life, and they heard the captain's muffled voice through the door.

"Who is it?"

"Ki and Jessica Starbuck. Please let us in."

The lock rattled as the bolt was thrown. "Come in, quick," the captain said in a hushed tone, opening the door. He stood aside in nightshirt and bare feet, a kerosene lamp in hand that cast eerie shadows off to the side.

Jessica tiptoed past the captain, a warm greeting in her large green eyes. Curt Bernard's crystal-blue eyes followed her into the room. Before Ki entered, he ushered Dr. Whitaker in. The chief of detectives stared in amazement.

"Oh, my gawd!" he gasped.

Chapter 13

After Ki, Jessica, and Dr. Whitaker detailed every moment of the last few hours, they finished the leftovers from Captain Curtis Bernard's dinner meal and some of the staples from the larder. The three had not realized how hungry they were until they began to eat. Suddenly they felt ravenous. Washing the food down with French wine, they settled down for the night.

Captain Bernard offered his bed to Jessica. He handed the men blankets, and he took the chesterfield. It would be cramped quarters for the night, but he was pleased to see the beautiful honey-blonde again—even if they weren't alone this time.

Ki positioned himself by the front door—just in case they had been followed, although he seriously doubted they had. He rolled himself into the blanket and dropped off into a light slumber. Part of him remained alert, ready to protect Jessica at a moment's notice.

Dr. Whitaker tossed and turned in his blanket, unaccustomed to such inconveniences. Finally their host got off the chesterfield and offered it to the surgeon. Without a word of appreciation, Louis Whitaker dropped down on the large couch and fell fast asleep. His body had not suffered this much exertion in years.

Curt Bernard, wrapping the blanket around him, lay near the back door, guarding his guests from the rear. But he found it difficult to sleep—not because of impending danger or disrupted sleep or the uncomfortable conditions. He could still smell Jessica's delicious fragrance. The knowledge that she was close kept him awake.

Finally unable to bear the strain any longer, he got up and tiptoed into the bedroom. He closed the door to the living room behind him and stood in the dark listening to her breathe. He inhaled deeply, filling his nostrils with her appealing, musky scent.

Approaching the bed, he whispered, "Jessie?"

"What took you so long?" she said huskily.

He heard the covers pulled back, and he stumbled to the bed, feeling his way along in the familiar territory. He pulled off his nightshirt and climbed in beside Jessie. Her bare flesh, smooth and warm, tingled on his as their bodies blended.

Curt took her in his arms and held her, kissing her on the nose and eyelids. As he ruffled her silken hair, he said, "I missed you. I really did."

"I've been thinking a lot about you, too." She cuddled in his arms, snuggling cozily. "Ummm, this feels so good— so right."

His lips sought hers, and they kissed deep and hard, their tongues playing erotic games. She shuddered with pleasure. Then Jessica slid down the length of the bed, kissing his muscular chest, licking the small nipple, sucking at his firm abdomen. She kissed and licked her way down to his manhood. Her lips and tongue greeted his nakedness as she moved ever closer to his maleness.

"What—?" Curt tried to ask.

"Just relax and enjoy. I learned this in the Orient, and I want to share it with you."

Her tongue flicked the head of his erection, and he squirmed and moaned. As she took it into her warm mouth, it was his turn to shudder. His body trembled as she took

128

more and more of him into her mouth, her tongue caressing the underside of him. Her hands kneaded his buttocks as the warm moistness of her mouth tantalized him.

"Oh, gawd help me!" he muttered, his head spinning with delight.

Jessie crooned with him in her mouth, sending vibrations up through him. Her hands squeezed him, and she bobbed up and down slowly. She could feel the tension in his groin tighten as he approached that point of no return. She kept up her leisurely pace, teasing his member.

Curt thrust his hips up automatically, writhing with pleasure. His hands wound around strands of Jessie's long hair as he felt himself build toward a climax. Her fingernails dug deep into his firm flesh as her tongue gingerly massaged his sensitive underside faster and harder. They both groaned passionately as they reached their fulfillment together.

Jessie's climax had mirrored his, and she lay with her head on his quivering inner thigh, breathing deeply and sighing in satisfaction. Curt reached down and pulled her up to him, holding her tightly in his arms. They lay in each other's arms again, cheek to cheek, and fell into a peaceful, dreamless sleep.

As daylight broke through the bedroom window, Jessie opened an eye and tried to focus. She was alone in the bed, and the welcome aroma of brewing coffee wafted into the room. She bounded from the bed and dressed quickly, looking for a water pitcher and basin to cleanse the sleep from her eyes and freshen her face.

Curt poked his head through the doorway and smiled dreamily at her. "Good morning, sleepyhead. Breakfast is almost ready. I've got fresh water for you here." He brought in a large pitcher of water, placed it on the bureau next to the big ceramic bowl, and padded back to the kitchen, leaving Jessie to her morning privacy.

During a breakfast of ham steaks and eggs, fried bread in butter, and coffee without chicory, the four plotted the capture of the Mad Ripper. Dr. Whitaker remained silent, since he realized he was in the company of professionals. He was happy to suggest alternatives when they gave him the opportunity, but he respectfully refrained from offering unsolicited advice.

"There's going to be a riot," Captain Bernard said soberly, "if we don't catch that murderous fiend soon. There are plenty of self-righteous idiots like Clark Buttrick out there, just waiting to make a name for themselves—or to cause trouble."

Jessie said, "Then why don't we go out and find the Mad Ripper?"

The chief of detectives cast her a cold stare. "And what do you think we've been trying to do?"

"No," she said, "I mean, *find* him—set a trap for him and catch him."

"Trap?" It sounded to Jessie as if all three men said it at the same time.

"Yes, a trap." She looked from face to face. "So far, he's been calling all the shots. And he hasn't left us much to go on."

The men nodded; Ki frowned.

She continued, "If he's attracted by ladies of the evening—let's give him one to go after."

Dr. Whitaker shook his head violently. "Jessica Starbuck, I don't like what you're suggesting. It isn't safe—he's not sane, and insanity is unpredictable. Besides, your father would have been against the idea."

"You're wrong there," Jessica shot back. "He'd be confident that I had learned enough from him to be perfectly safe. And I have Ki to help me."

Curt Bernard looked from Ki to Jessie. "You're saying

130

you want to go out there and lure him? Not on your life—the doctor's right. I won't allow it.''

Dr. Whitaker smiled. "You have a point there, Miss Starbuck. And you certainly are your father's daughter. You're quite right—that's just the kind of plan Alex would have thought up." He gestured to the captain. "Do you have a better plan?"

"No, but I refuse to permit Jessie to use herself as bait!"

"I won't be in that much danger, Curt. I'll have you and Ki and the whole police force behind me. And Ki and I have done this kind of thing before. Right?" She looked to Ki, her big green eyes pleading.

"This is true. Captain, Jessie can take care of herself. You should know by now just what an extraordinary woman she is. Anyway, I promised her father I'd watch out for her, so I would never let anything happen to her. You can count on that."

The honey-blonde took Ki's hand and squeezed it for reassurance, then took the captain's. "You both know I am the only one who can do this. With you keeping an eye on me, I will be fine—and we'll catch the slasher before he strikes again."

When the newspapers proclaimed the slayings of the fifth and sixth victims—the Reverend Arthur Bergendorfer and one of his soiled doves—people lined up twelve deep at the train station, all trying to buy tickets for anywhere outside St. Louis. Crowds mobbed each stagecoach out of town, and hysteria spread like butter on hot toast. Men packed up entire families and headed east; husbands and wives left everything behind and rode out of the city on horseback or by wagon.

The governor declared martial law, and troops from the St. Louis Arsenal flooded the streets each night, marching with rifles in hand, keeping order in the city. The newspapers warned that anyone out at night without the proper credentials or a pass from the governor or mayor would be arrested.

Ladies of the evening took to their rooms, seeing only customers they knew well—and many such women had already packed up and left the city. If Jessie were to pass herself off as a streetwalker in order to lure the slasher to his capture, she must do it in daylight hours. Even the slasher must be aware of the curfew, and any painted woman out near dark would be suspicious. It would be difficult to set a trap for the ripper that did not appear to be a trap.

When Chief Carstairs heard Captain Bernard's proposal that Jessica pose as a fallen woman to lure the slasher into action, he railed.

"Are you crazy, Curt!?" he yelled for half the building to hear. "Capturing the ripper is a job for the police department—not a couple of freelance detectives, one of 'em a woman!"

His head thrown back, Archie bayed in response to his master's volume. To quiet the hound, the chief scratched under the dog's chin. Archie's howl became a low growl and culminated in a deep yawn. He got up, turned around twice, as if looking for a comfortable place to lie down, and snuggled back at the chief's feet.

"Hell and damnation, Curt," Hiram Carstairs said between clenched teeth in an attempt to keep from setting off his hound again, "I realize our police force hasn't done all that marvelous a job of it—but a woman?" He put up a hand to interrupt the captain. "I know, she's a pro, and so's that Oriental."

"And we have little choice, Chief. When the first sporting girl was discovered with her throat slit, neither of us dreamed there would be five more deaths and martial law! Forget our jobs, let's just think of protecting the citizens of St. Louis from this raving lunatic. He must be stopped by any means at hand—and Jessica Starbuck and Ki are our last hope.''

Shaking his head in defeat, Chief Carstairs said, ''I'll have to talk to the commissioner first.''

The police commissioner agreed to the plan—especially since no one had offered a better one—and Chief Carstairs gave the order to put the decoy plan into action. The territory for Jessica to patrol was plotted. She would stroll from Delmar Boulevard on the north to Chouteau Avenue on the south, between First and Seventh streets. Although the slasher had strayed west to Union Station for his fourth murder victim, he had probably followed her from her home not far from that area.

Jessica and Ki, with Captain Bernard in tow, paid a visit to the Floating Palace. While the show in which Joy Madison had starred was closed down, another melodrama had taken its place. But Joy's costumes—some for the role of a cheap floozy—were piled away in a steamer trunk, along with her makeup and stage jewelry. Jessie appropriated everything and donned the gaudiest of the outfits.

Curling her long honey-blond tresses and piling them high atop her head, leaving one large curl to hang saucily down below her bosom, she applied the stage makeup heavily until she barely recognized herself in the mirror. When she entered the room in full costume and makeup, both Ki and the captain stared in disbelief.

''My gawd! Jessica?'' Curt Bernard was not certain this painted hussy was Jessie, although the large green eyes were there, peering out from behind clumped mascara and brazen eyeshadow. ''You look like . . . like—'' He could not find the words.

Ki could. ''Perfect!'' He beamed. ''Perfectly awful, but a perfect decoy.''

Jessie smiled, her garish makeup exaggerating her smile

133

into a grimace. "Let's hope he falls for this before he kills someone else."

"And let's hope he doesn't kill you!" Curt Bernard said somberly. "Now, the plan is for you to go out and saunter down the street, right? We'll be right behind you, ready to jump on him."

Jessie shook her head. "No good. If there are too many police around, he'll surely see them. Even the soldiers must be pulled away from my decoy area. This will work much better if only Ki keeps me within range at all times. Your men can be posted—out of sight—on the rooftops of the buildings I stroll by."

Ki said, "That might do it. If Jessica stays within that one square-mile radius, your men can stake themselves out in windows or on roofs. I'll stagger around with a bottle in hand—no one should pay much attention to me."

Jessie added, "And it will be plain to anyone who does look Ki over that he is completely unarmed, and therefore harmless. That will also work in our favor." She grinned at the captain. "Remember, Ki is more deadly unarmed than most men are when packing a number of weapons."

The first day Jessie paraded the streets as a harlot, she was accosted dozens of times by well-meaning brutes who sincerely wanted to hire her services. A drunk or two followed her, and one tried to snatch her handbag. She fended each off by herself, Ki keeping his distance. They worked smoothly as a team, each making circles around the other without appearing to. No one watching them would have suspected their collusion.

Feet aching in Joy's fashionably uncomfortable shoes, Jessie took to the streets the second day, covering more territory, but always staying within range of the policemen on the roofs and in the windows of the buildings she passed. Again she and Ki came up empty. No one even closely resembling the slasher's description approached Jessie.

134

On the third day Curt Bernard suggested she actually take someone to her rooms—rooms the police had rented for the occasion—as if accepting a customer. If the slasher had seen her, he might watch her pattern of action before moving in for the kill.

The chief of detectives assigned a military sergeant from the St. Louis Arsenal to play her customer, since the ripper just might be acquainted with the faces of the police force detectives. The rough staff sergeant gratefully played his role to the hilt, paying for Jessie's services on the street, then escorting her to her rooms.

They chatted awhile, then the sergeant left, adjusting his outer garments for effect. Minutes later Jessie returned to the street to walk her territory again. The shadows grew long, and the late autumn air turned chilly as Jessica made her last turn onto Chouteau Avenue.

She glanced around for any sign of customers, keeping her eyes from straying to the hidden riflemen on the rooftops. Ki stumbled by, singing raucously and waving his nearly empty bottle. Her back to the gray-brick wall of a building, she rested her feet as best she could by leaning against the wall. She stood on one foot, then the other, making painful circles with her ankles.

As she pushed off to continue her route, she heard a soft voice from behind her. "'Scuse me, miss, but how much?"

Jessie turned to see a tall older gentleman carrying a large new portmanteau. His dark coat hung almost to the ground, and his floppy hat nearly covered his eyes. The thick, striped muffler wrapped around his neck and face blocked everything from view but his long nose.

Her eyes wide, Jessie smiled brightly. "What'll you offer?" She noticed an odor that was familiar, but she couldn't place it. She stuck out her hand. "Hmmm, big boy? You make an offer."

135

The man stared, his dark eyes searching her face. "In advance?"

Jessie smiled sensuously. "It'll cost more when we get there. Two bits now—four bits later."

Ki staggered into a doorway, his ears straining to hear what was said. His muscles tensed and ready to pounce, he held his breath and waited.

The man dug deep into his overcoat pocket. A gloved hand produced two shiny coins. "Here. Now we go?"

Jessie tossed the coins casually into her handbag, her senses taut. This could be the one. He matched the description to a degree. He might be a little older than most of the people said, but he had on dark clothing. He was not as dapper and posh as witnesses described, but he might have changed attire to keep from alarming his intended victim.

The man extended his arm, and Jessie took it, hanging on to him partially from roleplaying and partially from tight shoes and painful feet. They were not far from her rooms, and she led the way. Not once did his hand move to open the portmanteau. In silence the two headed for her rooms as Ki circled nearby. Jessie kept up a steady stream of chatter once they reached the front steps. While she spoke, her mind raced as she tried to sense if this were the slasher. That strange but familiar odor bothered her, but so far he had not made a move.

Once inside she made a big thing of locking the front door behind her. She knew Ki had slipped in by the back door and would be waiting to pounce from the kitchen. She took off her cape and bonnet and eyed the customer provocatively. He averted his eyes and removed his gloves, keeping his hat, coat, and muffler on. He stuffed the gloves into his overcoat pockets and placed his portmanteau on the bed.

As he clicked the suitcase locks open, Ki's legs prepared to spring forward. This would be it—the man was going for his scalpel. Ki sucked in a deep breath of stale apartment air and poised to jump.

The man flung back the suitcase lid and reached under the clothing packed on top. Before he could bring his hand back out, Ki spun around, his foot knocking the portmanteau off the bed and setting the man off balance. Jessie and Ki each grabbed the man by a wrist and held him tightly.

"What are you—" he yelped. His eyes wide with fear, he trembled. "Please don't kill me. Take my money, but spare me, please!" he wailed.

Ki took both the man's wrists. "Get his case. See what's in it."

Jessie picked up the suitcase and put it back on the bed. She dumped the contents out onto the coverlet—clothing, toiletries, and a large corked bottle of Chianti. After sifting through everything twice, she asked, "What were you looking for in your bag?"

Terrified, the man looked from Ki to Jessica. His face pale, but with drops of sweat beading up on his forehead and above his mustache, he swallowed hard and remained silent, waiting to be killed.

Ki jerked his wrists. "Tell us!"

The man's mouth opened, but no words came out. His lower jaw sank, but he could not make words. He whined instead, his eyes rolling.

Jessie smiled. "If you tell us, we won't hurt you."

"For w-wine!" he managed. "I thought maybe wine would be good before—" He went limp and fell against the bed, whimpering.

Losing his patience, Ki demanded, "Haven't you read the newspapers?"

"No—I just get to America from Milano, from Italia. My bambini are in San Francisco, and I come to stay with them since my Giuseppina died. I get off the train for the afternoon, and I think it nice to celebrate my trip with

someone. But I know no one, so I hire this pretty lady."
He sobbed, his eyes rolling again. "Please, do not kill me.
Leave me some money or take it all—but do not kill me."
Completely frantic, the man broke into Italian, pleading over
and over again in his native tongue.

Jessica and Ki apologized for the rough treatment, urging
the immigrant to return to his train and wait to celebrate in
San Francisco. They helped him repack his case, and Jessie
gave him back his coins—adding some paper money as a
token of her regret for terrifying him. Since it was almost
dusk, they arranged for a police escort to take him back to
Union Station.

As the Italian left with the police, Jessie suddenly remembered that puzzling odor—raw garlic!

Although Jessica was approached several more times during the next few days, none of the potential customers fit
the description of the slasher. There had been no more
slashings, and Jessie's role did not seem to be attracting the
murderer.

The telegraph wires from Kansas City hummed. A young
lady of the evening had been found dead in her rooms—
her throat slashed and her organs removed and neatly lined
up alongside the body.

★

Chapter 14

Jessica and Ki wired the Kansas City police chief to expect them on the next train west. Captain Bernard himself sent a long, detailed wire explaining how the two planned to snare the Mad Ripper and requested any and all assistance from the Kansas City Police Department. Chief Charles Minty, all too glad to offer the services of his entire force, replied that his men were at their disposal, and he was readying them for Jessica and Ki's imminent arrival. Well aware of the hysteria that gripped St. Louis—Chief Minty knew the potential for panic his own city faced if the St. Louis slasher remained at large.

Chief Minty had heard of Jessica Starbuck and her companion—the Lone Star legend—and breathed a sigh of relief that such professionals would keep the local mayor and police commissioner out of his hair, and possibly even pave the way for his political ambitions. With great ceremony he made reservations for Jessica and Ki at the city's best hotel and awaited their arrival with extreme anticipation and the highest of hopes. If all went well, he would be able to take credit for capturing and executing the fiend that had terrorized and eluded St. Louis. And who knew where that would lead him—mayor? Governor? Higher yet?

In St. Louis, Chief Carstairs pulled strings to arrange for two sleeping-car rooms for Jessie and Ki, since every seat and compartment on all trains out of St. Louis had been

139

booked solid. The pair hauled Joy Madison's belongings with them, along with their own baggage. Since they knew the slasher to be in Kansas City, they both dressed comfortably for the short overnight trip. Jessica knew she would not need to don her fallen-woman decoy outfit until they arrived at their destination. Until then, they could enjoy themselves on the Silver Palace sleeper with attached dining car.

The train swayed, making it difficult for Jessie and Ki to negotiate the sleeping-car corridor as they made their way to the luxurious dining car for a bite to eat. While they had breakfasted at the hotel that morning, they had spent most of the day at police headquarters going over last-minute details with Chief Carstairs and Captain Bernard. They had barely enough time to get themselves and their luggage on board the train before it chugged out of Union Station.

As they sat side by side in the plush dining car, reading over the lengthy, gilt-edged menu, two burly toughs padded down the thickly carpeted aisle, passing through the ornate car on their way to the sitting coaches several cars forward. The men had come from the baggage car where they secured their horses. They planned to hook up with friends in Topeka who purported to be tied in with the infamous James gang.

As they ambled by, Ki and Jessie were too occupied perusing the menu by lamplight to notice the men look back at them. The one with big ears favored his right side, and the one with two front teeth missing limped badly. The two men glanced back in one of the huge wall mirrors and recognized the honey-blonde and her fighting companion as the two who had given them such pain in St. Louis. They would patiently wait in ambush for their revenge.

"I really don't care for that much food," Jessica said, pushing herself away from the table slightly, the rich, snowy-white linen napkin covering her entire lap. "The less

I have tonight, the better I'll sleep. I have enough trouble trying to sleep on trains."

Ki agreed.

The two ordered a light meal, which the waiter brought on fine china with great pomp. A crystal goblet of a rare French wine, a snifter of aged brandy, and a demitasse followed.

Leaving a mouthful or two of velvety dessert behind, Jessie stifled a yawn and stretched, admiring the elegantly inlaid woodwork and fancy wall-hangings. She felt almost at home. "I really am tired. I'll bet I'm asleep before my head hits the pillow—even on this train."

Ki tried unsuccessfully to fight back his yawn. "Me, too. We could both use a good night's sleep. Let's turn in." He yawned again loudly. "We can plan our strategy tomorrow over breakfast."

They headed down the wide aisle, passing diners still engrossed in their meals. As they reached the door to the platform leading to the next car, Ki pulled it open for Jessie, and she stepped into fresh air, a stream of steam and soot—and the waiting arms of Big Ears and Toothless.

Before Ki could get through the doorway himself, Big Ears picked up Jessie from behind, squeezing her in a vicious bearhug. Toothless lay in wait for Ki and tried to slam his fist into the Asian's face as he stepped out onto the platform. But Jessie's startled outcry alerted Ki, and the brawny tough's fist sailed by Ki's ear and crashed painfully into the wooden doorframe behind him. The man howled in pain, clutching his shattered left fist. Quickly Ki brought his knee up into the toothless man's crotch and the edges of his flattened hands down where the neck meets the shoulders in a crunching blow.

Toothless's knees buckled, and he toppled in a heap onto the open platform between cars. Rather than finishing off the unconscious tough with one deadly blow, Ki ignored him. Instead, he concentrated his efforts on Big Ears, who still held Jessie from behind, his massive arms crushing her as he dangled her over the edge of the train. He obviously intended to drop her off the hurtling railroad train. She held on to his arms, which threatened to take them both overboard if he let her go.

Ki sprang to Jessie's side, grabbing her arm as his foot swung around, delivering a flying *tobi-geri* kick to the bruiser's head. Big Ears's grip on her waist released as Ki's foot landed sharply, sending the tough reeling. Jessie's hand clasped Ki's wrist as she fell off the platform, her feet flailing in empty space. With no railing to protect them, they both nearly went over. Ki had his hands full trying to keep Jessie from falling, and Big Ears turned on them, his six-shooter drawn as he tried to keep his balance and shoot.

Ki yanked hard, pulling Jessie to safety. In the same motion he spun around, his body a blur to the eye. His foot connected with the revolver and sent it flying off into the darkness. Big Ears bellowed and lunged, but in midflight, Ki's fist chopped hard and caught him on the side of his head, just above one of his enormous ears. Dazed, the big tough staggered backward, waving his arms to catch his balance and right himself. Ki spotted the instability and took advantage of it, coming up from underneath, levering Big Ears completely off balance and out into space. The tough's angered cry diminished rapidly as the train sped on, leaving him far behind in the dark void.

Jessie stood watching, holding on to the doorhandle of the dining car to keep from falling off herself, relieved to have that behind her. Ki turned just in time to see a revolver pointed up at him. Jessie looked back and saw Toothless take aim at her. She had no time to react. Ki crossed his wrists in a *gedan-barai*, as if to fend off a blow, and yanked the gun from the man's hand as it went off. The bullet soared past the honey-blonde's ear an inch from its target.

Toothless jumped to his feet and came at Ki with both fists flailing, his face contorted, with what was left of his teeth bared in an animal-like snarl. As he hurled himself on the Asian, Ki sent a deadly *yonhon-nukite* thrust to the man's heart. Toothless literally stopped dead in his tracks, collapsing at Ki's feet. Jessie helped Ki dump the body off the platform into the darkness.

Not quite as sure of themselves as they had been when they first boarded the train, Jessica and Ki checked the *Silver Palace*'s corridor in both directions before entering their compartments for the night. As the two said good night and locked their sleeping compartment doors, they agreed they would definitely sleep well now, with such exertion to top off their meal.

The next morning, when Jessica and Ki awoke, they fully expected the train to be slowing down for its arrival in Kansas City. Instead, the conductor informed them that there had been a delay during the night—livestock on the tracks—and they were several hours behind schedule. After freshening up as best as possible on a train, they headed for the dining car and a light breakfast. They were still sitting over coffee when the train pulled into Kansas City's Union Depot.

Jessie and Ki watched the train station coming into sight from their vantage point in the elaborate dining car. As Jessie poured more coffee from the sterling silver server, Ki called her attention to the small newsboy standing on the train platform just outside their window.

A tiny paperboy ran alongside their car, not six feet from them, holding up the latest issue of the Kansas City *Star*, calling, "St. Louis Ripper Strikes Again!" The headline proclaimed the fiend's latest slashing. There had been another villainous mutilation in Kansas City. Ki and Jessie

143

looked at each other and shook their heads. The Mad Ripper was at it again, and they were too late to prevent this second vicious slaying. They hurried off the train and searched for their luggage.

Chief Minty, clad in his fanciest dress uniform and flanked by a number of uniformed police officers, greeted Jessica and Ki formally. They could tell by looking at him that this tall pompous man with an inordinately thick thatch of white hair under his gold-braided helmet with plume was ready to watch them find the killer and then take full credit for himself. His transparent motivation, while not lost on Jessie or Ki, mattered little, since there was a murderous lunatic to be stopped. They only hoped that this apparently pretentious old windbag's ego would not be a stumbling block for them.

Chief Minty's welcoming speech lasted far too long, his resonant baritone voice booming out, and seemed more aimed at the attendant members of the press and the audience than for Jessie and Ki.

". . . and in conclusion," the chief droned on, "may I say that we of Kansas City will all be indebted to you two if you help us to rid ourselves of the murderous fiend who has attacked our fair city and committed such heinous crimes against our women. Although we have everything well in hand and expect an arrest at any moment, outside assistance is always welcome in our ever vigilant effort to make Kansas City a better place in which to live."

Privately, when the audience had dispersed, he said, "Thank God you're here! We really need your help. We're stumped."

Before joining Chief Minty and his detectives at police headquarters, Jessie and Ki asked to check in at the hotel the chief had selected. A police escort took them to the Hotel Savoy, assuring them it was "KC's finest." They were guests of the city, with carte blanche. From this, the two sensed the desperation of the situation.

In their hotel suite, amid bouquets of flowers and baskets of fruit, Jessie and Ki took turns reading the newspaper accounts of the two brutal slayings. There seemed to be little difference from the six gruesome slashings in St. Louis, at least from what the city's two daily papers had to print. They would find out more when they met with the police.

After cleaning up and changing from their traveling garments into their working jeans and shirts, the two followed their escort to police headquarters by the quickest route possible. The patrolman who brought them could hardly keep his eyes off Jessica. Her lime-green, skin-tight shirt matched her large luscious eyes, and the six-shooter in her holster looked brand-new and very expensive. Impressed by these two, the young policeman hurried them as fast as he could. The pressure was on.

At police headquarters Jessie and Ki planned to stay just long enough to meet the chief of detectives and his men. After listening to what the police had found—or, rather, what they had not found—at the murder scenes, the two asked to be taken to where the most recent victim had been found.

Captain Jerry Ruzika, a wiry redhead in his early forties, seemed reluctant to share what little evidence he had with the newcomers. The freckles across his nose fairly danced off his face as his temper flared. A gigantic wad of chewing tobacco in his cheek distorted one side of his face and his speech. He spit, hitting the chief's brass cuspidor on the outer rim.

"Chief, I see no reason to bring in a woman and a—"

"Captain!" the chief interrupted. "Miss Starbuck and Mr. Ki are here as guests of the city—and they must be treated as such. We are to cooperate with them fully. Is that understood?"

Captain Ruzika's face turned even redder, more freckles popping out. He chomped down on the wad of soggy tobacco, let loose another foul-smelling stream that splotted dead center into the spittoon, and blustered hotly, "Damn it all, Charlie, I still don't think—"

"You never do, Jerry!" the chief stopped him again. It appeared obvious to Jessie and Ki that the captain was accustomed to being insubordinate and having his own way—and the chief had been fighting a losing battle with the younger man for quite some time.

Turning on his heel, Captain Ruzika motioned to one of his men. "Turner, you take Miss Starbuck and Mr. Ki wherever they want to go." To the police chief he snapped, "I have better things to do than babysit a female and a—"

"Dammit, Jerry." The chief smiled in embarrassment and held out a hand to Ki and Jessica. "Please excuse my men, and don't judge Kansas City by them. I'm sure Lieutenant Turner will show you whatever it is you need."

"Before we go, Chief," Jessica said, her eyes telling him she understood, "I want to let you know what we have planned. Chief Carstairs said he would fill you in, but I want to make sure you know exactly what we're planning to do to catch this monster."

She and Ki outlined their plan for trapping the slasher using Jessie as a decoy. The chief was reluctant at first to permit anything quite so foolhardy, but when Captain Ruzika insisted the ruse would never work, Chief Minty agreed to allow the plan to be implemented.

"There's a fiend running loose with a straight razor, slashing pretty women, and she wants to stick her neck out? All right," Captain Ruzika fumed, nearly choking on his tobacco wad, "let her go get her throat slit. Sounds fine to me. I can see the headlines now—'Guest of the City Slaughtered!' That should really go a long way to getting you

146

elected mayor, Charlie." He spit hard, this time missing the cuspidor completely.

"Enough, Jerry. Turner, please take Miss Starbuck and Mr. Ki to Charlotte Wingate's rooms at Mama Taggletti's. Now." The order came from deep down inside the chief, and the young police detective jumped.

As Lieutenant Turner escorted Jessie and Ki out the door, he said to them, "Please call me Howard, Miss Starbuck, Mr. Ki."

"Then you call me Jessie—and that's Ki, not Mr. Ki." She turned and smiled broadly at the chief and the chief of detectives as they left. She heard a splat and a muffled grunt as the door slammed shut behind her.

Lieutenant Turner found two sturdy horses for Jessie and Ki, and the trio rode off to Mama Taggletti's boardinghouse near the corner of Tenth and Broadway. Charlotte Wingate, the lieutenant explained, had been a fairly homely lady of the evening until two nights before, when someone slit her throat and removed her insides.

From what the lieutenant described, the murder scene seemed the same as all those in St. Louis. When they reined in their horses and tied them to a hitching post at the big red-brick boardinghouse, it began to rain. A late autumn shower drenched the three before they had time to make it to cover. They climbed the steps and knocked on the front door, glad to be under the cover of the house's eaves.

A large woman with a thick Italian accent answered the door. "Oh, Lieutenant Turner, hello." She greeted the ruddy young police detective as an old friend and looked at his two companions, waiting for an introduction.

"Mrs. Taggletti, this is Jessica Starbuck and Mr. Ki from Texas. They're here to help us find out who murdered poor Charlotte."

The stout peasant woman beamed and ushered the three in. "I'm so glad you come. We gotta find who done dis to

147

my Charlotte. Charlotte, she good girl. She no deserve dis.'' The woman's expressive face tightened in a grimace of pure sadness as tears welled up in her small dark eyes. She looked from one to the other. "I help, you help. We find the—" She lapsed into Italian, spouting forth a fountain of epithets in her native tongue.

Jessica said, "Yes, Mrs. Taggletti, we'll see what we can do for Charlotte."

The heavy woman huffed and puffed her way up the stairs to the rooms Charlotte had occupied for over three years. As she unlocked the door, she stood back, unwilling to enter the blood-spattered room. Keeping her eyes averted, she mumbled something about having pastry in the oven and returned to the first floor, leaving the police detective and his companions to examine the room for themselves.

Rain pattered against the windows as they lighted a big brass kerosene lamp to brighten the storm-darkened room. Deep splashes of dried blood scarred the room. Apparently nothing had been disturbed since the body had been removed. The murder victim's clothing lay strewn on the chair next to the bed, dark with her dried life's fluids. A basin of evaporating bloody water sat on the stand by the bed, pieces of muslin at the bottom. The murderer had apparently bathed himself after slashing his victim, Ki pointed out. This was part of his pattern.

Ki took up the lamp and dropped to his knees, searching every inch of the tattered rug and rough flooring for any clue or piece of evidence. Nothing.

Lieutenant Turner showed Jessica and Ki the back entrance to the rooms, where the Mad Ripper obviously entered and left without being seen.

He said, "One of Mama Taggletti's other tenants, Hannah Blanchard, saw Charlotte go up the back stairs with someone—a very wealthy-looking, average-sized gentleman carrying a little black leather case. She said she thought he

148

was a doctor but didn't think anything of it until after her friend was found sliced open. Then she remembered hearing something about the slashings in London and St. Louis.''

Jessica said, ''May we speak with the witness—Hannah, is it? There might be something she forgot to tell you initially. I'm sure you know how people remember things later, but unless asked, rarely come forward.''

''That's true,'' the police detective said. ''Unfortunately, Hannah packed up and left the day after the murder. 'Course, I don't blame her. I wouldn't stay around either if I was in her line of work and there was a madman thinning out my competitors.''

That evening, after the rain stopped and the moon and stars came out crisply in the autumn chill, Jessica wandered into the brisk Kansas City night air, her face garishly painted and her friend's floozy costume making the most of her shapely body. She avoided the still-muddy streets and kept to the rain-slogged boarded sidewalks.

Ki stayed in the shadows as Jessica Starbuck acted the decoy, looking every inch a strumpet. They hoped this would be the night they brought the Mad Ripper to his knees. He had to be caught before he decided to suddenly end his reign of terror and disappear forever. They knew that once he ceased his killing spree—unless caught in the act—he would be impossible to find.

As they expected, their first night out proved fruitless, just as it had in St. Louis. Dozens of offers, but no Mad Ripper. But they weren't worried; they were laying groundwork for the trap.

On the second night, after being accosted by several drunks, Jessie focused her attention on her sore feet. A tall man dressed all in black came up behind her and grabbed her by the arm. He pulled her to him and whispered raspily into her ear, ''Come with me!''

Startled, the honey-blonde smiled broadly and said in a feigned Southern drawl, "Anything you wants, dearie."

With the strength of four men, the tall stranger hauled her along, almost cutting off the circulation in her arm. He said nothing further but dragged his quarry quickly into the darkness of an alleyway. Their feet clattered on the rugged cobblestones and splattered in the puddles from the afternoon's shower.

Ki, dropping the whiskey bottle, swung around silently, following the two as a shadow. Employing the cover of buildings and debris in the alleyway, he used his *ninja* moves to keep from being detected. He kept Jessie and the tall man in black within sight, closing the gap as quietly as possible without being seen or heard.

The tall stranger in black had dragged Jessie out the other end of the alley, and Ki lost sight of them. He left the *ninja* moves behind as he sprinted for the mouth of the alley. As he rounded the corner, he heard Jessica scream out for help. Her cry came from somewhere across the street. She was being carried inside one of the large wooden buildings facing him. But which one? It was too dark to see very far, and there were too many doorways she could have been hauled into.

A heavy door slammed shut, its bang reverberating down the row of buildings in both directions. Ki could not pinpoint the direction of the slam. He only knew it came from across the street.

Ki ran from the alley into the rain-soaked street. Trying to cross the muddy thoroughfare, his moccasined feet sank deep in the mire, strong suction bringing him almost to a halt. He pulled himself slowly to the other side of the street, leaving his moccasins somewhere in the sticky slime, and dashed up the first short flight of stairs he came to. The door was locked. He pounded on it. Nothing. The windows were dark.

He rushed down the steps and to the next set of stairs. Up to the door in a flash, he banged and tried the lock at the same time. No answer. He went to the next building. Still nothing.

"Jessie!" he yelled in desperation. The echo of her name came back at him. "Jessie! Where are you!"

Then he heard Jessie again. Her cry bounced off the walls of the buildings across the street and sounded as if it might be coming from a building two doors down to the right. Ki jumped from the stairs and sprinted toward the echo of Jessie's cry for help. Hurtling barefooted along the sidewalk, he saw a light go on in the window of the building next to the one he had thought Jessie's cry came from.

He headed toward the lighted window and the massive door next to it. "If I'm too late," Ki said to himself in a hoarse whisper, "I'll kill him and then myself!"

Chapter 15

Jessica Starbuck's scream chilled Ki to the marrow as he took the steps of the building three at a time. He cared about nothing but saving Jessica—the woman he had pledged to protect, Alex Starbuck's only child, the shining light he had vowed to keep safe at all costs.

A failure! That's what he was! The *te* master could handle almost anything—his body was a living weapon. He had always felt invincible. But now Jessica Starbuck was in danger, and he had somehow let her down. He must get to her in time. That scalpel had better not have sliced her lovely throat!

Ki threw open the heavy wooden door and charged into the first room he came to, his bare feet slapping on the planked flooring. The darkness and silence that greeted him forced him to try another room. A familiar yet difficult to place odor assailed his nostrils, but there was no time to try to identify the smell. Ki ran to the next door leading off the hallway, flinging it open. More darkness. He stopped to listen and heard a loud masculine voice. It came from somewhere across the hall.

Ki sneaked down the hallway, attempting to avoid squeaky boards by sheer will. Following the deep sounds of someone almost yelling, he came to a door where the voice seemed the loudest. Pausing only a moment, he opened the door quietly, hoping the hinges would not screech and give him away. He found himself in an immense room. A small lantern glowed dimly off at the other end of the cavernous chamber. Jessie gasped, and Ki could see a tall, dark stranger—the ripper?—bending over her.

Swiftly, silently, and invisibly, employing the *ninja* moves again, Ki made his way toward the front of the room. As he did, a brighter light came on when the tall man in black struck a match and touched it to the wick of a large hanging kerosene lamp. The huge room filled with a yellowish glow, and Ki—poised and ready to rescue Jessica from her abductor—saw the pews and altar, and smelled the familiar odor of incense. It was a church!

"Repent, sinner!" the tall man intoned piously, threateningly. "Harlot! Strumpet! Slut! Release the demon within thee and repent!" The stranger, his cloak open and his clerical collar in evidence, shouted at Jessie. "Save thy soul, sister, before thee rot in everlasting damnation! Repent in the name of Christ Jesus thy Savior!"

Jessie lay sprawled at the far end of the altar where the ranting clergyman had flung her, causing her to cry out in pain. She raised her hand and called, "Ki, it's all right. He just wants to save my soul."

Ki lowered his arm and pocketed the *shuriken* he was about to throw. "Are you all right?"

"Yes, I'm fine. Just a little muddy and a lot unsettled. I had visions of scalpels or razors and spending my last moments in this dreadful costume."

The evangelist turned on Ki, his eyes widening at the sight of the tall, slender, barefooted Asian. "Heathen! Repent or ye shall boil in hell for all eternity along with the strumpet! Let Christ into thy heart—thrust out thy pagan ways! Repent!"

Ki ignored the zealous evangelist and rushed to Jessie's side, helping her to her feet. "Are you certain you're all right? Did he hurt you?"

154

Jessie nodded, rubbing her bruised wrist. "Yes, I'm all right, and no, he didn't really hurt me—just roughed me up a little." She winced at the tender wrist. "He certainly is a strong one."

"I can never forgive myself. This is all my fault. You might have been—"

"But I wasn't. I'm fine." She glanced down at Ki's bare feet. "What happened to your moccasins?"

"They're stuck in the mud in the middle of the street. Let's get out of here—we've had enough for one night."

As they turned to go, the evangelist dashed for the entrance and threw himself flat against the door, blocking their way. "No one leaves the house of the Lord until they repent!" he boomed.

Jessica dipped into her handbag and pulled out a gold coin, a double-eagle. She handed it to the zealot, saying, "Is this repentance enough, Father?"

The tall evangelist's mouth sagged open as he stared at the twenty-dollar coin in his hand. Meekly, he stepped aside, his attention focused on the shiny coin. Their captor temporarily distracted, the woman and the heathen got away.

At the hotel the two very muddy, disheveled patrons tried to gain entrance but were blocked at the front door by an indignant clerk who instantly sized them up and barred them. In all the commotion and exhaustion, they had forgotten their attire. They had left by the servants' entrance, and they should have returned the same way. Contritely, they allowed themselves to be hustled out. On the street they sneaked in the back way and up to their rooms.

After a long relaxing soak in a tub, Jessica dressed for dinner. Ki, shining from his tub, followed. They dined in the hotel restaurant and listened to the other diners tell one another of the frightful whore and the filthy savage she tried to bring into the hotel for a sexual romp. They all agreed it was brazen . . . simply audacious. Jessie and Ki smiled at each other.

Early the following morning Jessica and Ki reported to police headquarters and asked for Lieutenant Turner. The young police detective came out to greet them and gave them directions to the site of the first mutilation. This victim, Clara Felding, had rented a room by the month in the Mandrake Hotel in the worst part of town. She brought all her customers there, although she lived in a small boardinghouse two blocks away, preferring to keep her professional and personal lives completely separate.

The police had already questioned the night clerk at the hotel when the body was discovered, but there might be something new he remembered. It would be worth a try. Unfortunately, Lieutenant Turner explained, his home address was not in the police file. The night clerk on duty at the time of the slaying would probably be at home asleep, but perhaps the day clerk could give them the address. The lieutenant apologized for not being able to go with them this time and gave them detailed directions to the Mandrake Hotel.

Jessie and Ki reined in their horses in front of the ramshackle hotel. It was indeed in a disreputable part of town. The toughs lounging on wooden chairs out front and in the hotel lobby made the crowd at the Red Fox Saloon in St. Louis look like gentlemen.

As the honey-blonde and her tall companion entered the lobby, all eyes bored into them. One shaved-bald bruiser sporting a long, mangy reddish beard and sweeping dark eyebrows sidled up to the desk, blocking Jessie's way. She moved to go around him, but he shifted with her, still barring her from the desk.

"Excuse us," Ki said, trying to get by the bald tough ahead of Jessie.

156

"For what?" The big bruiser scratched his chin through the whiskers. "What'cha done that we gotta 'scuse ya for, huh, chink?"

Throwing back his head, the bearded bully howled with laughter. His raucous amusement encouraged others, and soon all the toughs laughed scornfully at the couple invading their territory uninvited.

After looking over both Ki and Jessie, the bald thug sneered and spoke to his drunken friends. "Look—the chink ain't got no gun—no knife. Unless he's got sumptin' sneaky up his sleeve, the stupid cuss ain't got no weapons. But this here blondie is packing, though." He laughed from the gut, still blocking Jessica's path. "Boys, I bet she's his chink-squaw! See—she's got a fancy six-shooter. What d'ya wanna bet she does the chink's fightin' for 'im?" He threw his head back again and nearly choked laughing.

Ki tried to ignore the toughs. To the desk clerk he said, "Could we ask you—"

The bald bruiser shoved a meaty fist against Ki's shoulder. "You ain't askin' nobody nothin'! We don't allow no chinks in here!"

The tough next to the bald one blocked Jessie and Ki's way, too. He looked like a derelict and smelled like a mountain man. "Yeh, Butch is right. The squaw kin stay, but the chink's gotta go." He reached for Jessie's buttocks and squeezed with both hands.

Jessie jumped, drawing her six-shooter as she leaped. Ki grabbed the bald bully's fist and twisted the man up and over. The big bruiser landed flat on his back with a loud "Ooofff!" as Jessie kept everyone else covered.

Someone behind Jessie moved, but Ki's *shuriken* sliced through the air and slit the tough's arm at the bicep. The thug yowled as his arm dropped to his side, useless. Ki spun around and delivered a quick *tobi-geri* kick to the derelict's temple, then sidekicked the tough rushing in to

157

help his mates. A short bruiser aimed his head at Ki's middle and tried to ram him, but the *te* master sidestepped the little thug and sent a *choku-zuki* blow to the little fellow's throat. The tough staggered and toppled, unable to breathe.

"Excuse me," Jessie said to the hotel clerk as she edged around the fighting, "I just have a couple of questions to ask, and we'll be on our way."

Ki levered another tough over the desk with a "Look out!" to Jessie. Although she had the thugs covered, Ki had everything well in hand. He spun again, cracking the ribs of the bald thug who had recovered enough to get to his feet and lunge at Ki.

Keeping one eye on the action, the desk clerk twirled his handlebar mustache and leaned toward Jessie. "What d'ya wanna know?"

"We need to speak with the night clerk who was on duty when Clara Felding was murdered. The police don't have his address. We thought you might know—"

Another drunken bully sailed by Jessie on his way to the other side of the desk and unconsciousness.

Leaning away from the fighting, the clerk said, "That'd be Eugene Rimov. He's got a room at the same place the other sporting girl lived—over at Mama Taggletti's on Broadway. He'll be in after midnight tonight—he works from twelve to ten."

"Thanks." Jessie pointed the six-shooter at the ceiling and fired twice. Gaining everyone's attention, she smiled daintily. "Thank you, gentlemen, for the warm reception, but my friend and I must leave now." She looked around at the human wreckage on the floor and behind the desk. "Sorry we couldn't stay longer."

The two mounted their horses and headed off toward the boardinghouse. Mama Taggletti recognized them and welcomed them back to her humble establishment. "It is good to see you again. I am just putting up some coffee—you have a cup with me, no?''

"Thank you, no," Jessie said, smiling appreciatively. "We'd like to speak with one of your boarders, Mr. Rimov. Which is his room?"

"Oh, that is such a shame." Mama Taggletti looked crestfallen. "He leave on the train yesterday. He tell me his mama sick; he gotta go. He pay me for whole month, say for me to keep the rent." She searched their faces for recrimination. "I try to give it back. He make me keep it. He good man."

Jessie nodded. "Yes, I'm sure he is. He must have been in a quite hurry. Could we please see his room? That is, if you haven't cleaned it yet."

Shaking her head, Mama Taggletti grinned. "Not yet." Pointing to the back of the house, the pudgy landlady took out her keys and led them to the room. "He say he get telegram at work. Must go to mama now." She opened the door.

Ki entered, but the drapes were drawn, and it was too dark to see anything from the glow of the gaslight in the hallway. Mama Taggletti lighted a handlamp and gave it to Jessie, who held it high as she went in. Ki flung open the drapes. All over the bed, scattered on the floor and the dresser top, were clippings from the Kansas City *Star*, as well as from many of the St. Louis papers. It appeared as if the night clerk had a collection of articles on the Mad Ripper. The odor of stale newspaper and unwashed laundry hit them hard as they read through the night clerk's collection of clippings. Two of the clippings had words underlined—*Mama Taggletti's boardinghouse* and *the Mandrake Hotel*.

On the dresser Jessie found two large bone hairpins. She held them up for Ki to examine. "What was he doing with these?" she asked.

159

"More to the point," Ki responded, "who do they belong to?"

"And why did he leave in such a hurry? Or, rather, why didn't he leave sooner?" Jessie looked around the room, picking up clippings to look under them. "Why wait an additional day? He's the clerk on duty at the hotel when the first girl is found. Then he's here at the boardinghouse when the second girl is killed. Perhaps he saw the murderer, knows who it is, and has to leave before he's the slasher's next victim."

"I wouldn't doubt it in the least," Ki said. "If only we had come here sooner—or known about him when we were here the first time." He slammed his hand down hard on the dresser top. "Why didn't the police tell us about him when they sent us here in the first place?"

"That's a very good question." Jessie took another look around and headed for the door. "Have you seen enough here? I think we should get back and ask the police some questions, don't you?"

Mama Taggletti backed out of their way just in time to keep from getting herself trampled as the two stormed out of the night clerk's vacated room.

As they brushed by, Jessie said, "Thank you, Mrs. Taggletti. If Mr. Rimov contacts you, or if you think of anything else relating to the case, please let us know. We're at the Savoy Hotel downtown."

The two rode back to police headquarters in silence, each deep in thought about what they had found. Eugene Rimov's disappearance was a little too convenient, and the police had a some explaining to do.

At headquarters Jessie and Ki headed straight for Chief Minty's office. Ki flung open the door without knocking, and the two walked in to confront the police chief.

The pompous white-haired man stood up from his desk, wringing his hands. He appeared to already know what they

160

were going to say. Captain Ruzika stood next to the desk, chomping on a wad of tobacco and glaring. Ki and Jessie waited to hear the chief out, but his news took them completely off guard.

"We just got a telegraph message from Omaha—the Mad Ripper struck there last night."

Chapter 16

Ki and Jessie packed as quickly as possible and arranged to have their luggage taken to the Kansas City Union Depot. They purchased their tickets in advance for the three o'clock to Omaha, again buying space on the Silver Palace for another overnight journey.

The Mad Ripper seemed to be one step ahead of them all the time. If they were to succeed with their plan to trap him, they must be in the same city as the slasher. Their frustration mounted as they waited for the train. They had let the Kansas City Police Department know exactly what they thought of the ineptitude of a force that allowed two key witnesses to slip through their hands and out of their city.

They wired the Omaha chief of police to let him know they were on their way, and headed for the train station. As the train for Omaha pulled into the depot, their conductor pointed out their compartment and had a porter carry the luggage onboard. Even the luxury of a plush sleeping compartment could not calm their anxiety—trains were too slow. They must get to Omaha and catch the killer.

Jessie glanced at her gold lapel watch. ''It's nearly four o'clock. If this is the three o'clock train, it's late.''

Ki smiled at her impatience.

''Why is it trains are never on time?'' she asked, her

frustration mounting. "Why can't trains and stagecoaches be early?"

Ki laughed to relieve the tension. "They're only on time when you're late, and they're only early when you have an important connection to make."

"I'll drink to that! In fact, let's have an early dinner and get a good night's rest."

After settling into their rooms, they headed for the dining car. The train gave a lurch as they started down the corridor, and the train station melted into the distance. Jessie and Ki held on to the window railings and the compartment wall as they made their way to the dining car. Neither of them minded the rocking of the train, since it meant they were that much closer to Omaha and the ripper.

Even before they reached the dining car, the delicious aromas from the kitchen assailed their nostrils, whetting their appetites. The waiter, splendid in his cutaways and white gloves, greeted them at the door to the dining car and offered to escort them to a table.

Ki said, "Opposite sides of a table for two—in the middle of the car." He planned to make sure they were not ambushed again.

While Jessie read the menu, Ki kept an eye on the door behind her and, through the wall mirror, on the door behind himself. Then it was Jessie's turn to watch while Ki chose from the menu.

Many leisurely courses later, they returned to their sleeping compartments and went to bed early. Sleep did not come quickly or easily. Both of them had too much pressing on their minds. Finally the rocking of the car and the clack of the wheels lulled them into a fitful sleep.

The following morning, the train pulled into Omaha's Union Station as Jessie and Ki finished their morning meal. After such a long sleep, they both felt the need for a hearty breakfast. They watched the station pull into view as they sipped the last of their coffee.

The foot traffic had thinned considerably by the time Jessie and Ki left the train. A flood of immigrants from Europe had poured out of the day coaches carrying battered and crude luggage; they wandered onto the station platform, looking for a familiar face. Those from the Silver Palace cars carried fine luggage and strode off purposefully.

Jessie and Ki waited for a police greeting, but none arrived. After the last passenger off the train had departed the station, it was obvious they were not going to be officially met.

"Do you think they didn't get our telegram?" Jessie asked, looking around.

"Who knows. Let's check into a hotel and then find out what happened."

They told a cabbie to take them to the best hotel in town and asked where police headquarters was located. The cab driver pointed out city hall and police headquarters as they passed by.

"Is there anything new on the Mad Ripper?" Jessie asked, impatient to get the investigation started.

The cab driver looked back at her blankly. "What Mad Ripper?"

"The one who's been terrorizing St. Louis and Kansas City. The one who killed someone here the other night— that Mad Ripper," Ki said.

"I don't know about no Mad Ripper, ma'am, but there were a killin' t'other night. But it were just some whore what got her throat slit, that's all. Ain't no problem here in Omaha—we ain't got no Mad Ripper." He laughed.

"Oh," Jessie said, looking at Ki. A block farther they pulled up in front of a luxurious-looking building.

After cleaning up and unpacking, Jessie and Ki went to police headquarters and asked to see the police chief.

165

The desk sergeant said, "Just a minute. You got an appointment?"

"We wired the chief we were coming. Jessica Starbuck and Ki. Please let the chief know we're here."

The police sergeant sent a note back and received an immediate response. "The chief'll see you now." He pointed off down the hall. "Third door on your right."

Policemen in uniforms, and those in civilian clothes, poked their heads out to catch a glimpse of the honey-blonde beauty in the skintight jeans and body-hugging shirt. Jessie could feel eyes probing into her as she and Ki headed down the hallway.

At the third door on the right, Jessie burst in without knocking, with Ki on her heels. She tread on a plush oriental rug, thick and luxuriant. Two chairs of dark crimson velvet stood in front of an oversized mahogany desk, and seated in a huge dark-maroon leather chair behind the desk was a bearded man with a full head of curly black hair. His clenched teeth held the largest stogie Jessie had ever seen.

He'd be almost handsome if his eyes weren't so cruel, Jessie thought as she looked the bearded man over.

"Thank you for seeing us. I am Jessica Starbuck, and this is my associate, Ki." Jessie reached over the gigantic desk and extended her hand to the bearded man.

"Yes. I got your wire." He took her hand, shook it limply, and dropped it. "I am Edgar T. Grogan, Omaha's chief of police and police commissioner." He grinned broadly, the cigar never moving. "Now, what can I do for you?"

"We're here because of the slashing. We've been tracking the Mad Ripper ever since St. Louis." Jessie watched the chief blow smoke rings.

"Why would you be wantin' to concern yourself over something that really ain't of no import?" The chief puffed blue foul-smelling smoke toward Jessie and Ki. "It was just

166

some slut gettin' her due, that's all. Why would anybody be gettin' all in a dither over a few sportin' gals bein' weeded out?''

"I'm sure the Omaha papers also mentioned the ripper murdered the renowned actress Joy Madison—"

"Actresses be just one step above a whore!"

Jessie stared in disbelief. "But Chief! There's a vicious murderer out there mutilating young women. Their morals aside, they are human beings. He's already killed seven women—and a man of the cloth!"

Creating another blue cloud and several tiny rings, the chief sneered. "Any preacher what mixes with sluts gets what he deserves." Thumbs in his bright green velvet vest, he tapped his fingers proudly. "Besides, that weren't here. We ain't got no problems here in Omaha."

Ki could barely believe his ears. "Then you won't mind if we take a look at the murder scene—since there's no problem here?"

"Now, where'd you get the idea that you can come bargin' in here from Lord knows where and take over?" He chomped on his stogie, bringing ashes down on his expensive vest. He concentrated on cleaning himself off before looking up. "No, you cain't see the murder scene. In fact, I'm sure you'd have a much better time in Omaha if you spent it at the train station on your way to somewheres else."

Jessie's huge lime-green eyes darkened to an almost forest green as they narrowed, her long lashes lowered. She stared straight into the chief's small dark eyes, sending a message he could not miss.

How could I have ever thought he was handsome! she thought in disgust. "Thank you so much for your warm hospitality, Chief Grogan. Ki and I will not soon forget it," she said with exaggerated politeness.

Ki slammed the door as they left, and Chief Grogan's

hollow laugh chased them down the hallway. They strode down the long corridor in silence.

"Pssst! Please, over here." A young policeman poked his head out from a doorway and beckoned to them. "Quick, in here."

Jessie and Ki slipped into the sparsely outfitted cubicle and shut the door behind them. The young man's wide hazel eyes looked at them earnestly, almost pleading with them.

"You're Jessica Starbuck and Ki, aren't you?" he asked in a hushed tone.

"Yes," Jessie answered with a smile. "That's right. And who are you?"

"I'm Jedediah Eisenbauer, and I'm the one what sent the wire about the slasher." His hazel eyes darkened as he looked from Jessie to Ki. "It was my friend Daphne Delacorte what was murdered. She may have been a lady of the evening, but she was a lovely young gal. And the chief ain't gonna do nothin' about it." He tugged nervously at the fine strands of his blond muttonchop. "As far as Chief Grogan's concerned, the world would be a better place without ladies of the evening." His eyes teared up. "But he didn't know Daphne."

"Would you take us to the murder scene?" Ki asked. "There may be something we can do to help."

"Of course."

Jessie and Ki left police headquarters and waited at the corner for Lieutenant Eisenbauer to join them. It was a short walk over to Tenth Street and the slum hotel where Daphne Delacorte entertained her customers and met her tragic end. The police lieutenant led the way.

"Hey, there, Otis," the policeman said to the desk clerk, "how about lettin' us have the key to Daphne's room. Police business." He extended his hand.

The wizened old hotel clerk stroked his scraggily little mustache and twitched his right eye. "Naw. Won't do you

168

no good, lieutenant. The room's been cleaned slicker'n a whistle. You kin look iffen you'd care to, but there ain't nothin' to see."

His hand still out, Lieutenant Eisenbauer said, "How about lettin' us be the judge of that."

Otis reached back and grabbed a key from the hook numbered 213. "Good luck."

Jessie and Ki went through every corner of the room, but the desk clerk spoke the truth—the room showed no sign of violence. The sharp smell of lye lingered.

Ki said, "This room looks like someone went out of his way to clean it. I bet this room is cleaner than before Daphne checked in!"

Jessie nodded. "Something's wrong here."

The police lieutenant agreed. "Let's go. Otis was right."

As he handed the desk clerk the key, he shrugged his shoulders.

Otis said, "Well, I told ya, didn't I? Chief Grogan made sure it were clean!"

Jessie and Ki looked at the policeman, who shrugged again.

At the hotel Lieutenant Eisenbauer said, "I'll pick you up first thing in the morning, and we'll check on any witnesses we might have overlooked."

"Till tomorrow." Jessie smiled warmly.

After dinner Jessie dressed in her harlot outfit, and she and Ki made the circuit of the streets of Omaha. Aside from the usual dozen or more offers from lusty men, there was no sign of the slasher. None of the potential customers looked the least like the murderer. Jessie's feet hurt, and Ki tired of staggering in circles around her. They had purposely not told the young policeman of their decoy plan, since they felt it would be better if he knew nothing.

Empty-handed and discouraged, they returned to the hotel by the back way, having learned their lesson in Kansas City.

The next morning, while they sat at breakfast in the hotel dining room, Lieutenant Eisenbauer rushed in.

"I really wanted to help you capture the slasher, but I guess I won't have the chance," he gushed, completely out of breath.

Jessie waited a moment while the young man calmed himself. "Why not? What's happened?"

His hazel eyes gleamed. "There's been another slashing—in Cheyenne!"

Ki repeated, "Cheyenne? When?"

"Last night. Can you beat that? Last night!" He shook his head incredulously. "It came in over the telegraph wire this mornin', and I was the one who had to take it in to the chief." Pulling at his muttonchop, he continued, "Well, I guess that lets the chief off the hook."

Jessie nodded. "Yes, and now his record is clean—just as clean as Daphne's room."

Ki said, "And I have a sneaking suspicion that the Mad Ripper got off the train just long enough to find and kill Daphne—and then got right back on the train. He didn't even spend the night here."

Jessie called for their bill and signed for it. She and Ki invited the police lieutenant back up to their suite, since to return to police headquarters would jeopardize his position. Once in the suite, Jessie pulled out a large map and spread it on the low table in front of the chesterfield. The three gathered around it.

"St. Louis, Kansas City, Omaha, Cheyenne—straight along the Union Pacific route." Jessie looked up, first at Ki, then at the young police lieutenant. "He's headed for San Francisco!"

"Whadda'ya wanna bet!" the blond policeman yelped, unable to hide his excitement. "You're gonna catch him, ain't ya!" His hazel eyes shown brightly.

"Yes, we are." Ki's large black eyes glistened as he

smiled. Determination set his jaw as his lips spread into a grin. "We'll get him in Ogden!"

Jessie nodded. "We had better catch him before he gets to San Francisco. Once he's there, he's lost to us forever. That place swallows people up. You're right, Ki. We must stop him in Ogden."

Jedediah Eisenbauer shook his head. "But what if he did what he done here—what if he got off the train just long enough to slit some gal's throat and got right back on the train? He'll be in Ogden by the time you get to Cheyenne. He's one stop ahead of you."

Jessie smiled. "Yes, but the train he's on has to stop at every station, and it's on a schedule—of sorts. But if I remember correctly, I own a bank here in Omaha."

Lieutenant Eisenbauer stared at her, puzzled. "What does a bank have to do with train schedules?"

Ki smiled at Jessie. "Are you thinking what I think you are?"

"Of course! There's only one way to get to Odgen in time to catch that murderer—we have to put together our own train." Jessie jumped up and headed for the door. "You coming? I've got to get to the bank."

The young police lieutenant sat staring as Ki got up to follow Jessie. "But—what do you mean, 'put together your own train'?"

"Simple," Jessie said, motioning for him to join them. Without missing a step, she continued, "All trains are made up of engines, sitting cars, sleepings cars, dining cars, and such. Well, with money from my bank, we'll get an engine or two and a hotel train."

Ki added, "It won't have to stop at stations to pick up or leave off passengers, and it should be able to make good time with no baggage cars or freight cars to hold it back. It'll highball it all the way from Omaha to Ogden, stopping only to take on water."

Jessie nodded. "While the slasher's train stops at every station along the line, lugging heavy freight cars and coaches, as well as sleeping cars and dining cars. It has to stop to take on water, just as do we. But we don't have to stop to take on the mail or passengers. We should be able to make up a great deal of time between here and Cheyenne, and then even more from Cheyenne to Ogden."

Ki smiled. "It'll be a race, but I'd put my money on us."

Jessie grinned. "Especially if the engineer and firemen are offered a fat bonus to catch the slasher's train before it leaves Ogden."

Jedediah Eisenbauer looked stunned. "I heared about you two, but I never thought I'd live to see you in action. This is more than I could have imagined! Who'd a thunk you could put together a whole train! By golly, I'd put my money on you two any day!"

"We had better win," Jessie said grimly. "There are a lot of young women out there putting up more than money—their lives are at stake!"

Chapter 17

Jessica Starbuck and Ki introduced themselves to the president of the First Nebraska Bank and presented the letter of unlimited credit from the Circle Star account. In a matter of moments the situation was set.

"The bank owns its own hotel train—sleeping car, dining car with kitchen and smoker, and one of the finest, fastest engines ever built," the bank president boasted. "And Brewster Harrigan's the best goddamn chief engineer this side of the Mississippi—and possibly even on t'other side, too."

Ki said, "Then we better assemble its crew and get going. We have a train to catch."

Jessie shook the bank president's hand and led the way to the station. Their luggage had already been transferred from the hotel to the private train, and the seven-man crew stood ready to leave as soon as Jessie and Ki arrived.

Jessie told the chief engineer, "There's a bonus of fifty dollars each above your wages if we catch the train to Ogden—and double that if we get there ahead of schedule."

Brewster Harrigan whistled through his shaggy red whiskers and shook his head appreciatively. "Ach aye! You must be in a true and terrible rush." His chest puffed out. "That there is a generous offer if ever I heard one—and more so, cuz our crew'll pocket the whole hunnert. We're that good, we are, and never you fear."

Ki said, "Before we get moving, I suggest we give the crew our special instructions so there's no questions or confusion later."

"Ach aye, sir." Harrigan spoke quietly to Baskin Shumway, the silver-haired conductor. "We'll all be here in a moment."

Jessie led the way to the dining car and seated herself facing into the car at the first table. Ki stood next to her, a tall Asian sentry. One by one the crew trotted in and came to a halt in front of Jessie's table. The conductor formally announced each as he arrived.

"Curly Martin," Shumway intoned, "fireman." The balding man with grimy hands and face bowed slightly and waved. "Harvey Morrison, brakeman." An older man in stiff uniform and gigantic biceps grunted. "Jerome Fiddlemeyer, relief engineer-brakeman and all-round handyman." A barrel-chested young man grinned at them through a few yellow-green teeth. "Horace Washington, porter."

Jessie and Ki remembered the large black man and greeted him warmly. His eyes shined in recognition.

"Nehemiah Williams, chef and waiter. The best blessed cook in this whole country." The slender black man smiled humbly and nodded.

Jessie explained their mission with a simplicity of terms, and Horace Washington nodded his assent.

"Ma'am," he said, "I'd do this fer nuthin'—jes' to catch that murderin' loony."

The porter seemed to speak for them all, and they dispersed even before Jessie had finished. They were all business, and there was a train to catch.

As the chief engineer headed forward, he called back, "Ach aye, this here beauty'll do a good forty-mile-an-hour standing on her ear. Push the darlin' and she'll gi' me up to fifty or more." He grinned proudly. "We call her the *Sandy Star*, y'know." The door slammed shut behind him, but Jessie and Ki could hear his cheerful, melodic whistle all the way to the engine.

Ki said, "The *Sandy Star*—for Alexander Starbuck?"

The conductor shook his head. "Never a man. No, we named her after Mrs. Starbuck, but we didn't know her first name."

Jessie was touched. "Thank you. My mother would be honored."

With a jerk and a lurch, the train moved, leaving the Omaha train station far in the distance within minutes. Jessie and Ki could feel the power of the great engine as it pulled its light but luxurious load.

By noon the *Sandy Star* sailed past one whistle-stop after another, its horn tooting a hello and good-bye as it barreled along. Harrigan was right, the train could really move. Ki reflected that if they kept up such a searing pace, they might make it to Cheyenne in less than twenty-four hours instead of the normal thirty-six.

Chief Carstairs patted Archie's head, and the hound looked up at his master and licked the gentle palm lovingly. The St. Louis police chief knew his wounded dog had long since recovered completely from the shooting, but he could not bring himself to leave the dog at home. First, he feared another attempt might be made on the dog's life, and losing his third hound to some vengeful maniac would be more than he could endure. Even more important, the police chief had grown accustomed to having the hound at his heels.

Ignoring the mayor's demands, Chief Carstairs made one excuse after another for keeping Archie with him at police headquarters. The dog seemed to feel right at home wherever his master went, and the policemen at headquarters looked upon Archie as a member of the force.

Chief of Detectives Curtis Bernard stood at Chief Carstairs's desk, his fists clenching and unclenching. "We should have heard something from Miss Starbuck and Ki before this." The light-haired captain slammed a fist onto the desktop. "Dammit it all, Chief, I should have gone with them!"

"Hell and damnation! They'll catch the sonuvabitch, don't worry about that none." The chief puffed at his pipe, blowing the smoke away from Archie. "They're on the move again, I bet. Last stop was Omaha, wasn't it?"

Captain Bernard nodded. "Now, about that Clark Buttrick. He's in hiding after him and his band of thugs tried to bushwack Dr. and Mrs. Whitaker and Jessica and Ki." He paced to the end of the desk and back. "But one of my sources knows where he is. I think we can bring him in this time and put him away for a good long while."

"Well, don't just stand there—do it!"

"Yessir!"

Captain Bernard called for his group of elite detectives and a handful of uniformed policemen. They armed themselves well for the raid on Buttrick's hideout. Slipping in from both ends of the street, the police swarmed over the riverfront warehouse and cornered Buttrick in a loft.

At first Buttrick planned to shoot his way out, yelling he would never be taken alive, but after counting the number of policemen Captain Bernard had brought, he thought better of it and tossed out his gun.

Hands cuffed behind him, he was marched out of the smelly warehouse unceremoniously. Two of his men, both in agony from festering wounds, gave little resistance and seemed almost relieved at being captured. At least, they reasoned, their infected wounds would be treated before they were hanged. And if they got a lenient judge—they might get off with a short term in jail. Being a vigilante had not been as much fun as they originally thought.

Putting up a belligerent front, Buttrick threatened the

captain. "You just wait till I get my strength back. There ain't no jail what kin hold Clark Buttrick!"

"Oh, shut up!" the captain said in disgust. "You can tell it to the chief. I don't wanna hear any more of your horsecakes."

At police headquarters Buttrick again set up a verbal barrage. "Clark Buttrick ain't gonna stay here long! Do you hear me!"

"Gawd, the whole territory hears you! I hope they hang you just to shut you up!" the captain shouted over Buttrick's railing.

The desk sergeant came around to assist the captain and his men, since Buttrick was kicking and yelling. The other two toughs, energized by Buttrick's antics, also began to yell and kick.

Buttrick, carried away by his men's reaction, swung his knee up and into the captain's groin, sending the chief of detectives into a paroxysm of agony.

"That's it!" the captain gasped from the floor. "I have had enough of you, Buttrick!" He shouted to the sergeant. "Release his cuffs. It's about time I teach this sonuvabitch a lesson!"

The sergeant stood there. "Captain, let's get him in a cell first. How about it?"

"Now, sergeant! That's an order!"

The two toughs hooted as the sergeant unlocked Buttrick's cuffs and backed away. The police might have six-shooters and rifles on them, but their pal would make Captain Bernard regret his decision. They cheered for Buttrick, ignoring the armed policemen who stood over them.

His hands released, Buttrick came out swinging. The captain danced around him, his fists poised in proper boxing fashion. Buttrick laughed and kicked Captain Bernard in the kneecap. The policeman stumbled and lurched to the right. Buttrick brought a left hook up from the floor into

177

the captain's jaw, sending him flying into the heavy waiting-room bench.

Before the captain could get up, Buttrick rushed over and kicked him in the ribs. Everyone could hear a sharp snapping noise as bones cracked. The thugs cheered, and the policemen cocked their guns. The captain staggered backward but caught himself on the edge of the desk and pulled himself around.

With all the power he could muster, Captain Bernard swung his fist into Buttrick's face. Blood spurted everywhere from the bruiser's broken nose. This time the police cheered.

"You goddamn—" Buttrick hollered. He rushed the captain, head down.

Bernard brought both fists up under Buttrick's chin and sent him flying. He stumbled into the crowd of onlookers, who tossed him back to the captain.

Buttrick lunged at Captain Bernard, grabbing him by the neck and choking as hard as he could. The two men fell to the floor, each holding the other's throat in a death grip. When it appeared that neither would release his grip, the sergeant stepped in and hauled Buttrick off the captain.

The thugs hooted and booed, yelling for the sergeant to keep out of it.

Fists flew and blood flowed. Chief Carstairs ran from his office to see what the commotion was. He stood with his mouth open as he watched Buttrick and Captain Bernard pummeling each other.

"What the hell is going on!" he demanded.

Sergeant Laymon yelled over the noise of the two brawlers, "Captain Bernard's fixing Buttrick's wagon, sir. No problem."

"Looks to me as if they're both getting the worst of it. Hell and damnation—stop it!"

The two ignored the chief, beating each other bloodier

and bloodier. Buttrick's fist connected with the side of the captain's head, and the policeman staggered back. As Buttrick raised his fist to follow through, he stopped dead in his tracks, staring past the police chief.

Archie, his hackles raised and his fangs bared, growled so ominously that everything quieted suddenly. All eyes fell on the hound as it stood there, ears back, front legs apart in the attack stance.

Before anyone could react, Archie bounded for Buttrick's throat. The bruiser fended off the lunge with his arm, but the big hound grabbed Buttrick's wrist in his sharp teeth and ground down to the bone.

Buttrick howled in agony. "Get him off me! For crissake, get him off! I'll sue the stinkin' police department! Get the damn dog off me before he kills me!"

Sergeant Laymon ran past Chief Carstairs and grabbed at Archie's collar. The hound resisted, his viselike grip on Buttrick's wrist unyielding. The harder the sergeant pulled, the more the dog's teeth ripped. Buttrick screamed in pain, kicking at the dog.

Chief Carstairs yelled, "Archie! Heel!"

The hound immediately dropped his hold on the thug's wrist and padded obediently toward his master. Buttrick pulled back his foot and kicked the dog in the hindquarter with his heavy boot.

As his boot landed a crunching blow, Buttrick growled, "I shoulda made sure you was dead, you mangy bastard!"

Chief Carstairs yanked his revolver from his holster before Buttrick finished speaking. "You sonuvabitch! You shot my hounds!" He aimed at Buttrick's heart.

Several policemen yelled at the chief to stop, and Captain Bernard jumped at the chief's arm. But Archie was quicker than anyone. He leaped at Buttrick's throat again, and this time his fangs sank in, severing the carotid artery, ripping the thug's throat out.

179

Chief Carstairs motioned everyone to let Archie be. The police kept their guns leveled on the other two toughs while the hound brought Buttrick down. When the bruiser lay still, Archie licked his chops, and with a pleased yelp, bounced back to stand at his master's heel.

The police chief patted his dog's head and said, ''Good boy, Archie, good feller. You men clear this garbage out of the lobby.''

Each member of the train's crew had his own sleeping compartment. They spelled one another in shifts; the *Sandy Star* never stopped for anything but water. All the stations and depots along the way had been telegraphed to watch for the highballing hotel train. Tracks were kept clear, and sidings were made ready. Everyone was only too willing to cooperate with Jessie and Ki.

Each telegraph agent had also been given a description of the slasher with a request to hold anyone who even remotely resembled him and to wire ahead to have the train flagged down immediately.

The *Sandy Star* sailed by town after town, averaging a little over forty miles per hour. The crew had their water stops down to a science, and everyone pitched in to make each mandatory stop as short in duration as possible. If Brewster Harrigan and his crew kept up the pace, Jessie and Ki would be in Odgen when the ripper's train pulled in.

Their only worry was whether or not the murderer was indeed on the way to Odgen. As they shot past Cheyenne, they hoped they were correct.

Chapter 18

Jessica Starbuck kept in constant contact with the station-master in Ogden, Utah. When the passenger train from Omaha arrived, a number of railroad agents and policemen watched as people left the train. Immigrants, families moving west, businessmen, and travelers—none matched the description of the ripper.

Jessie also kept in close touch with stationmasters at all the train stops between Cheyenne and Ogden, just in case the ripper left the train before Utah. As the hotel train hurtled by each stop, the telegraph reported no one disembarking any train who remotely resembled the slasher.

Ki said, "He either stayed on the train in Ogden, or he's slipped by us somehow."

Ki stretched out his long legs and looked across the smoker section of the dining car at Jessie. Half the car had been made into a luxuriously comfortable sitting room, and Ki and Jessie were joined by Baskin Shumway, the hotel train conductor.

Jessie shook her head. "We'll know soon enough." She glanced at her lapel watch. "Harrigan says we should be in Ogden within half an hour—before the passenger train leaves the station for San Francisco."

Conductor Shumway beamed at them. "Harrigan's as good as his word. He said he'd get us to Ogden before the passenger train left, and he will."

Jessie smiled. "Even if Harrigan couldn't make it, I asked the Ogden police to hold the train until we arrive. If the ripper is on that train, we have him."

Twenty minutes later the *Sandy Star* chugged in to the Ogden train depot, pulling up right behind the passenger train. Police and train officials greeted Jessie and Ki as they jumped to the platform.

After a thorough search of the train to assure themselves the ripper could not possibly be hiding there, Jessie and Ki accompanied the police to headquarters. Jessie explained their plan to trap the ripper.

The police chief balked. "I won't have you murdered in my jurisdiction, Miss Starbuck. Your reputation aside, that ripper's insane and slippery as an eel. He'll slit your throat and nick out of town before you're finished bleedin'!" His fat cheeks turned a bright pink.

Ki and Jessie finally persuaded the police chief to allow them one night's masquerade. The entire police force could be stationed on rooftops if need be, but Ki and Jessie assured the chief they could manage alone. They set their plan into action.

Out on the street in her garish harlot's costume and full makeup, Jessie sidled up Washington Boulevard to Twenty-fourth Street, causing a great deal of consternation among the primarily Mormon population. Ki kept to the shadows, making *ninja* moves, since a drunken Asian would call too much attention in such a sparsely populated town.

One family man after another accosted Jessie to berate the slut in their midst. Their attitude disheartened her, and she feared they might chase away her target.

As Jessie crossed Washington and strolled down Grant Avenue, a moderately tall figure stepped out of the shadows and approached her—hat brim pulled down and coat collar up, wide muffler obscuring the face, with fancy suede gloves carrying a gleaming leather physician's satchel.

182

Jessie's heart leaped as the stranger's husky whisper breathed warm air into her ear. "May I join you, pretty lady?"

"Oh, you startled me!" she said honestly. She looked up at the stranger, trying to see beyond the thick muffler and hat brim. Jessie feigned a flashy Southern twang, adding authenticity to her garish appearance. "I haven't seen you 'afore, dearie. You ain't from around here, are you?"

"No, I just got in. I'm between trains."

"Oh? That's funny—I was jes' down to the train station, and I didn't see you get off," Jessie lied, probing. She felt a chill run through her as she watched the stranger open a gloved hand. There were three shining silver dollars. "For me?" She took the coins and dropped them one at a time into her string handbag. "How grand. Let's get in outta the cold, why don't we?"

"Yes, let's."

Jessie felt certain she had the ripper this time. This one fit the description perfectly. But there was only one way to make sure—she had to be attacked. Her pulse pounding, she took the stranger's arm and headed down the street, knowing that Ki would see and stay close by.

She led her customer to the Hotel Ogden and along the poorly lighted corridor to room 12. She and Ki had arranged for the room in advance, and giggling coyly, she held out the latchkey for the stranger to unlock the door, delaying long enough to give Ki time to get into place through the window off the alley.

"Are you a doctor?" Jessie asked, looking down at the leather satchel.

"A surgeon."

Jessie noted great pride in the response. There was something familiar about this tall stranger, but she could not put her finger on it. She lighted the table lamp next to the door and watched her quarry go straight to the dressing screen

183

and step behind it. If this really was the ripper, she reasoned, he would undress completely before attacking her. But how did he get off the train unnoticed? she wondered.

Jessie hesitated a moment, then unbuttoned her blouse and skirt. Although she kept her back to the screen, she could see everything behind her in the mirror over the chiffonier. She saw articles of clothing being folded and draped over the top of the screen. As she took her time removing her own costume, she tried to see the man's face. But the hat stayed on with the brim pulled down.

"Come here, beautiful."

Jessie approached the screen, still working on her unmentionables.

"Turn around. I have something for you."

Jessie turned, confident that Ki—who she knew would be hiding in the alcove next to the window—could stop the ripper before she became another slashed victim. She heard the satchel click open, and she braced herself for Ki's imminent rescue.

Suddenly Jessie cried out as she glanced at the window and saw Ki outside in the alleyway, struggling to open the locked window! As she spun around, she saw in the mirror the raised scalpel come down at her. She ducked and jumped out of reach, just in time to see the ripper standing there in front of the screen—stark naked.

"Priscilla!" Jessie yelled. She stared at Priscilla Whitaker's boyish nude body, scalpel poised. "Oh, my God! You? You're the ripper?"

Dr. Whitaker's ex-wife stood staring at Jessie, puzzled and confused. "How do you know me, whore? Who are you?" The tall, lanky young woman lunged at Jessie, swiping wildly with the scalpel.

"Priscilla, it's me—Jessica Starbuck!" She ripped off the false eyelashes and beauty mark as she sidestepped the attack. She rushed for the window and released the lock.

184

Ki climbed through the window and stopped short. Out of instinctive modesty, Priscilla grabbed her cloak and threw it over her unclad body, covering her flat breasts and narrow hips. In two steps, he clasped her wrist and wrenched the scalpel from her strong hand.

Priscilla Whitaker's knees sagged, and Ki helped her to the bed. She sat on the edge, sobbing quietly. "Why did you have to stop me? My plan was perfect . . . perfect!"

Feeling a small twinge of compassion for the rejected wife of a famous surgeon, Jessie asked softly, "You know we had to stop you. Why did you do it?"

Priscilla opened her small, dark eyes wide. "I did it to prove how good a surgeon I am—and to rid the world of the women who steal husbands." She looked from Jessie to Ki. "Don't you see? I'm doing the world a service." Tears rolled down her cheeks and her lip quivered. She spoke more to herself than to Ki and Jessie. "They wouldn't let me in to medical school, you know, and I was a better surgeon than any of the men. Far better than my husband could ever hope to be. I proved that!"

She shook her head, a bone hairpin falling out and her thin brown hair tumbling down her back in wisps. "I never wanted Louis to be accused—I just wanted everyone to acknowledge my surgical abilities. Do you understand?"

Ki and Jessie nodded. They both realized how far from reality this woman had strayed. And now she would have to be brought back to stand trial. More than likely, she would be judged insane. She would spend the rest of her life in an asylum.

Ki said, "Well, at least we know how the ripper eluded everyone at the train depot. No one was looking for a woman!"

Jessie stepped into her skirt and buttoned it. After she finished dressing, she suggested Priscilla get dressed. But Priscilla refused to do so until Ki left the room.

Jessica nodded to Ki, saying, "It's all right. I can handle things."

Ki said, "I'll be outside the door." He unlocked the door to the hallway and stepped out.

As the door closed, Priscilla jumped up and turned the key in the lock. Before Jessie could stop her, Priscilla grabbed the little black satchel and slammed the corner of it into Jessie's head, sending her staggering. She swung again, hitting Jessie on the temple. The honey-blonde collapsed to the floor, unconscious.

"Stop me, will you?" Priscilla muttered as she took another scalpel in hand and bent over Jessie's motionless form.

The shiny instrument glistened as she brought it down to slice Jessica Starbuck's throat. The metal was inches from flesh when Ki yelled through the window.

"Stop! Don't do it!"

For a second Priscilla looked up, then brought the scalpel down in a slashing motion. A blur of shiny metal and a splash of scarlet squirted up. Blood spurted and gushed as life flowed out. Deep burgundy-red blood covered Jessie's pink flesh, dripping down to saturate the cheap rug.

As Ki climbed through the window, Jessie moaned and rolled over. She sat up and saw Priscilla Whitaker's lifeless body lying next to her on the floor, her throat torn out by Ki's *shuriken*.

From the Ogden train station, Jessie wired both Lieutenant Eisenbauer in Omaha and Captain Bernard in St. Louis:

RIPPER DEAD STOP BRINGING HOME LAST VICTIM
STOP SEE YOU SOON STOP JESSICA STARBUCK

186